HAWK

'So,' Gates said, 'what's your favorite sport?'

'Baseball, why?'

Gates nodded as if he already knew the answer, and opened the slow-moving cruiser's back door. 'Baseball,' he growled. Someone handed him a bat.

Hawk moved away warily as Gates hefted the length of wood, sighted along it, took a couple of practice swings, smacked it loudly against his palm.

'Sorry,' Hawk said, 'I meant Ping-Pong.' His face hardened. 'Listen, I'd rather go back inside than whore for you, you –' He stopped, slapped his pockets, snapped his fingers. 'Oh, I need to borrow ten bucks.'

Gate_____ __is head and came toward him.

H_____ ___ _he prison wall behind him
a_____ _____ _hat would help him climb
b_____ _____ _ only visible guard delib-
e_____

'Help_____ ___weakly. 'Police!'

T__ _____ __ ___

_____ __mly, just great. They're
n_____ _ou need them, and when
the _____ _'re not here anyway. What
the _____ y coming to, anyway?

he_____ he swung the bat at his

HUDSON HAWK

Geoffrey Marsh

NEW ENGLISH LIBRARY
Hodder and Stoughton

Grateful acknowledgment is made for permission to reprint
lyrics from the following song: SIDE BY SIDE by Harry
Woods. Copyright 1927 Shapiro, Bernstein & Co., Inc., New
York. Renewed. Used by permission.

First published in the USA in 1991 by
Jove Books by arrangement with Tri-
Star Pictures

First published in Great Britain in
1991 by New English Library
Paperbacks

A New English Library paperback
original

British Library C.I.P.

Marsh, Geoffrey
Hudson Hawk.
I. Title
823[F]
ISBN 0-450-56270-0

Printed and bound in Great Britain for
Hodder and Stoughton Paperbacks, a
division of Hodder and Stoughton
Ltd., Mill Road, Dunton Green,
Sevenoaks, Kent TN13 2YA (Editorial
Office: 47 Bedford Square, London
WC1B 3DP) by Clays Ltd., St Ives plc.

Long ago, the Duke of Milan commissioned a young artist to erect a mammoth statue of a horse. The time was 1481. The artist was Leonardo da Vinci.

This statue, the "Sforza," was to be the largest bronze statue ever built. However, weeks before the model was to be cast, war broke out and the Duke needed his bronze back for helmets, swords, and cannons.

Da Vinci would not wait for the Duke's bronze. He would create a machine, a machine to change common lead into the much-needed bronze.

When da Vinci turned his machine on, it was to give him something more than he expected . . . much more than bronze.

1

The sun lay such a gentle glow on the country-side that Enzio Gramaldi decided that it could only be duplicated in heaven. Plus a brilliant sky almost too painful to look at, a rainbow of beautiful blossoms flecked across the low hillsides, ancient olive trees twisted and green in their orchards . . . it was simply too much for a man of his romantic sensibility to take.

He smiled.

He clucked at his mule and eased it to the verge where, with a grunt, he dismounted. The mule stared at him. Gramaldi patted its neck—*hang on, old girl, I'll just be a minute*—and pulled from a bundle on the mule's haunches a small wooden cask. Then he found himself a seat on a lightning-blasted tree stump. An arrangement of clothing, a deep sigh of satisfaction, a sweep of hat from his head to the ground beside him.

It was warm.

His face, more like the side of a granite mountain, relaxed.

The mule snorted, twitched its tail, and wandered into the grass for some serious afternoon grazing.

Another sigh, and the merchant closed his eyes, brought the cask to his lips, and drank.

Life was good.

Actually, life was damn good. His wares sold in every village between Milano and Roma, his women were uncomplaining, and thus far he hadn't been waylaid by the thieves who often plagued the roads. He couldn't ask for anything more.

A muffled sound opened his eyes.

He grinned.

Ahead of him lay a huge building, a veritable castle no prince could ever hope to own, complete with turrets and high walls, flags and pennants, sunlight glinting from the mica in the stone as if every inch of the place had been inlaid with diamonds. To own such a home, Gramaldi thought; Lord, to own such a home!

He drank.

The mule ate.

He drank again, deeply.

And the urge to break into song, something loud and lively and deliciously lewd was almost too great to bear. Temptation filled his lungs, opened his mouth, and was instantly buried by a monstrous explosion that sent birds shrieking into the air, the mule into Switzerland, and the wine all over Gramaldi's clothes.

"Leonardo, *che passo . . .*"

Gramaldi shook his fist at the castle, at the window from which great gouts of smoke billowed, and at the mule, which had evidently decided that Switzerland was too far away, and besides there was too much good fodder here to pass up.

Sometimes, the merchant thought as he tried to swipe the wine from his chest, Da Vinci just went too damn far.

Which was a thought Leonardo da Vinci had himself as he batted his way through the clouds of smoke that filled a castle room large enough, it seemed, to house a small village and most of its scrawny livestock; one of these days he was going to blow the whole place up. The windows soon drew most of the smoke away, leaving behind a foglike haze. He coughed, muttered to himself as he pulled at his beard, and flinched when a sudden bright flash of light exploded in his face. Quickly he slipped a pair of sunglasses from his sleeve, blew on their tinted lenses, and put them on.

On the other hand, he thought with a satisfied smile, if the place blew up, so would . . .

It.

He paused.

He smiled.

The machine that took up fully half the wall and a good portion of the stone-block floor was almost too complex for the eye to comprehend. One could only see it in pieces, sections, in segments that defied description and fostered awe. Or, in the eyes of the hapless apprentices trying to shoo the smoke away from the structure, not a little bit of fear.

There was movement and cast shadows; levers and axles, globes and cylinders, mirrors that caught

• 3 •

the sunlight and sent shafts of vivid color slanting through the smoke as if they were beams from a manic laser; knobs and buttons and slides and things Da Vinci still hadn't had time to name yet bristled from every angle.

And yet it was beautiful.

Diabolical, perhaps, or perhaps even divine.

But it was beautiful.

And, he thought proudly, it worked.

Sort of. He had been commissioned by the Duke of Milan to cast a huge bronze statue of a magnificent horse called Sforza. Then the war had come, the commission had gone, but he had discovered that his means of making bronze in such large quantities had turned into the means of making something else.

Something altogether quite different.

"Basta, vapore," he commanded, his voice not loud but heard just the same.

Immediately, one of the apprentices manhandled a stubborn lever and a hissing plume of steam reached for the vaulted ceiling.

The machine slowed.

Da Vinci reached to a table and picked up a pair of tongs, clacked them open and shut to be sure they worked, then moved forward.

The apprentices backed away.

Da Vinci adjusted his sleeves, wiped a touch of nervous perspiration from his brow, and leaned forward, peering at a trough almost hidden among the slats and arms and gleaming brass of the machine. Behind the trough was a crystal, faceted and of such complexity—much like the machine itself—that to stare at it for very long brought tears to the watcher's eyes. Below it was a gold demon's head, smiling, and from whose mouth poured what appeared to be a gold river of light.

Da Vinci hesitated.

The demon grinned at him.

With a deep breath to calm himself, he slipped the tongs into the light.

One of the apprentices gasped.

Da Vinci frowned but said nothing. Instead, he drew the tongs away, in their grasp a bar of yellow from which tendrils of smoke curled.

There was silence.

Nothing moved.

Then the apprentices edged forward, murmuring, some smiling, others fearful.

"Maestro," one of them declared, *"che meraviglia!"*

The others agreed that what he had was fantastic, amazing, something unique and marvelous.

That what he had done was no less than a miracle.

Da Vinci looked at the bar still gripped by the tongs, looked at the faces of his workers, and suddenly realized what he had really done. No exercise, no intellectual game.

Something quite different indeed.

"Lasciatemi, solo," he said.

No one moved.

"Solo!" he ordered.

As they ran from the room, bewildered but not daring to risk questioning his command, Da Vinci turned away from them and stared blindly at the wall.

What have I done? he wondered. A shiver made him roll his shoulders. What have I done?

He stiffened and whirled back to the machine, and using the edge of his cloak, he snatched the crystal from its place behind the trough and hurried out of the room without looking back, almost running through the tapestried halls until he reached his private workshop. The doors slammed shut behind him.

For several seconds he struggled for calm, eyes closed and hands at his sides. When equilibrium returned, he wandered through the cluttered room, not allowing himself to think, just looking at all the work-in-progress for some clue, some hint of what he had to do next.

The crystal vanished into one of his pockets.

His hand moved then, gliding over the tables, the desks, as if searching for something new to hold. It paused for a moment, then followed the lines of a newly completed equestrian statue; it hovered over a quill pen upright in its inkwell, as if it were ready to jot something down in the large volume of sketches beside it; it drifted over a wood model of a strange flying machine with rotors atop its cabin, before he grunted and moved on.

A little painting, perhaps, he thought, something I can really concentrate on.

In the corner, on a stool, sat a lovely woman beside her portrait. He stared at it, complete save for the mouth, then turned to the woman, who smiled a greeting, revealing teeth that wouldn't have been happy in Enzio Gramaldi's old mule.

I have got to do something about that, he thought

glumly as he shook his head; some kind of paste, perhaps, or olive-flavored paint.

He nodded to her and moved on, out onto a balcony that overlooked a verdant valley.

So lovely, he thought with an almost overwhelming melancholy, so lovely, and so simple, and so filled with danger.

At that moment a bat-winged glider swooped out of the sun and past the balcony. Aboard was an apprentice who waved, nearly fell, and whooped as he guided his craft around the corner and out of sight.

Da Vinci smiled.

That ought to keep the damn chickens awake.

Then his hand brushed against his pocket and the smile faded into concern.

He pulled out the crystal and glared at it, nearly threw it away, then changed his mind and twisted it until it came apart and revealed nestled inside a tiny mirror. His temper flared and he folded each piece quickly and held them up, amazed, in spite of his anger, at how, in their current configurations, no one would guess what their true purpose was.

And no one ever will, he decided.

But again he could not bring himself to destroy the crystal utterly. That would be too much.

A look over his shoulder into the workshop, a slight nod at a thought that began to grow somewhere at the edge of imagination, and he leaned against the balcony wall and studied the valley beyond the wall.

Maybe, he thought, I won't have to deal with this at all.

Maybe . . .

A faint cry made him look up, and once again he smiled at the glider casting its shadow over the land.

Like a hawk.

The smile broadened.

Just like a hawk.

2

A shadow drifted lazily over the rooftops, the trees, barely noticed by those down below, definitely noticed by those smaller birds who appeared to be the target of the hawk's aimless hunting. They scattered, calling frantic warnings to each other, either diving into foliage too thick for the predator to follow, or trying to lead him away from their vulnerable nests.

The hawk flew on.

Its shadow cutting over the sun-caught Hudson River, rippling over the ruffled surface of the water, gliding onto the shore and back over the trees.

And still there was panic. One small bird, protecting its nest, charged up to meet it, but the hawk merely banked and flapped its wings once.

Unhurried.

Moving on.

Its shadow now drifting over a high stone wall topped with razor wire and electronic sensing devices, drifted over a deserted yard and past barred windows, drifted over a thick metal door.

And vanished.

Inside, in a large room noted less for its stark decor than its meaning, Eddie Hawkins stood patiently. There was no sense making trouble now, but he couldn't help checking the door just to be sure they hadn't moved it since the last time he'd seen it. He wouldn't put it past them. For ten years he'd been in this miserable place, mopping floors, working the laundry, doing his best to keep his nose clean, and listening then as he did now to the sounds of the prison guards snapping orders as if they were drill sergeants, cell doors creaking open, clanking shut; the infernal intercom system that produced more static than words; muted radios tuned to rock stations that produced music he barely tolerated, much less understood.

He sniffed and watched the overweight uniform come out of a storeroom with a bundle in his arms.

Hawk grinned.

The uniform ignored him.

Hawk wanted to kiss him. That's exactly what he wanted—for people to pay him no attention at all. If they had ignored him at his last job, he wouldn't have been in here in the first place. After all, he wasn't a huge guy, or an especially pretty guy, or a particularly muscular guy. He was a guy. People weren't supposed to pay any attention to guys. How the hell were guys supposed to make a living if people kept paying attention to them all the time?

The uniform dropped the bundle on the counter. "Okay," he said. "One coat, one hat. Some personal items. There's your wallet. I think you'll find everything in there."

Hawk held his breath for a moment as he stared warily at the clothes he'd last worn a decade ago. They were teasing him. They were going to take back his parole, he just knew it, that's the kind of luck he had; they were going to taunt him with his stuff, then take it back and grin.

"Trick or treat," they'd say, and back he'd go.

Inside.

The uniform looked at him, bored and uncaring. His expression said, *well, you gonna take it, schmuck, or do I gotta burn it?*

Hawk picked up the coat, slipped into it, and looked at the hat.

"Haven't seen one of those in a long time," the uniform said.

Hawk lifted an eyebrow. "Like that, Skeeter? Keep it."

Quickly then he picked up his wallet and checked through it, finally opening the plastic inserts to a photograph of a small monkey. He smiled, put the wallet in his pocket, and walked away.

"Hey," the uniform called, "you got to sign for this. Don't you want the receipt?"

No, he thought, I don't want to sign for anything in this damn place ever again. But thanks for asking.

The door was still there.

Sonofabitch, I think I'm gonna make it.

An adjustment to his coat, and he turned just as a door opened behind him.

Oh, well, he thought, nothing's perfect.

The man who approached him was sleaze on

rubber soles and a grungy trench coat to match. Hawk, in a former life, would have probably gotten the chair for what he wanted to do to this man; in this life, however, he knew that this toad was part of the reason he was now walking toward that door.

That one.

The one that led outside.

The man fumbled in his coat for several seconds before pulling out a set of keys. "So," he said cheerfully, "the great Hudson Hawk is finally getting out. Hey, remember all the reporters that were here when you came in? The world's greatest cat burglar. Now who gives a fuck?" He snarled at all the keys, the one he was searching for obviously not cooperating.

Hawk didn't offer to help.

There were, after all, limits.

When the uniform vanished back into his storeroom, Gates unlocked the door and looked at Hawk, eyes narrow, lips working before he said, "I got a proposition for you."

The checkpoint door opened and Hawk slid through before the man could change his mind. "The answer's no, Gates."

He hurried on without seeming to do so, gaze on the door he now saw in the distance.

The last door.

The Big Door.

He ordered himself to be cool. There wasn't anything out there he hadn't seen before; it was just ten years older, that's all.

Gates scurried to keep up with him. "Now listen, smartass, as your parole officer, I've found you a job."

Hawk shook his head. "No way."

Gates ignored him. "It's a terrific job." He lowered his voice, as if the guards high up on the wall would be able to hear him. "An auction house. One night's work, man, and you're free like no ex-con's ever been. No checking in with a shrink, no community service—"

Hawk smiled at him politely, without warmth. Not even through the Big Door and they were already after him to do something stupid. The man was nuts. "I *want* to do community service. I *want* to teach the handicapped how to yodel. I *ain't* stealing anymore, Gates."

Gates sneered. "Look at you, huh? Ten years later, you're still impressed with yourself. Same old coat, same old hat. You're extinct, Hawk, out of style."

They reached the Final Door, and Gates began fumbling with the keys again.

"Coming from you," Hawk said, eyeing the man's coat and hoping it wasn't catching, "that's a powerful statement. Aren't you supposed to *stop* me from committing crimes? You know, 'Book 'em, Dano.' 'Give a hoot, don't pollute'?"

Gates dropped the keys back into his pocket.

Hawk prayed for strength, maybe a lightning bolt. A localized earthquake would do in a pinch.

The parole officer grinned at him smugly, rocked back and forth on his heels. "You ain't out yet, wise guy. I can set you up and send you back anytime I want. It's a very fine line between an ex-con and an escaped con."

That's it, Hawk thought; push, and ye shall receive.

"Gates, Gates, Gates," he said. "Go fuck yourself."

While Gates waited for him to begin quaking in his shoes and beg forgiveness for his smart mouth, he took out his Pez dispenser, clicked it open and shut a couple of times, then turned his back and inserted it into the door's massive lock. Within seconds, the bolt turned over.

Still got it, he thought joyfully, the man's still got the touch.

He opened the door and stepped out, kicked it shut behind him, and stepped into the first free air he'd breathed in what felt like a million years.

"Hey, goddamnit," Gates shouted behind him. "Hey, I'm not finished talking to you, you little son of a—"

Without looking back, Hawk fluttered the man's keys over his shoulder, then tossed them into a trash can by the entrance.

Gates began to scream bloody murder.

Hawk began to whistle as he slipped his hands into his pockets and tried to decide where he'd go first. A glance at the prison, and he knew it was no contest—anywhere but here, and no loitering, please.

He laughed silently.

Hello, world, it's good to be home.

Then he heard the door open, and a police car pulled up, siren off but lights flashing.

Hawk moved on without hesitation.

The car followed.

He prayed that jaywalking hadn't become a capital offense.

Running footsteps then, and hoarse panting, and

he wondered if the Supreme Court had done anything positive about justifiable homicide. He glanced at the patient cruiser, heard Gates catching up, and muttered, "Why am I getting the feeling that getting out of prison is going to be a big fucking mistake?"

Nobody answered.

That figures, he thought, the only thing that hasn't changed in ten years is my goddamn luck.

He walked.

The cruiser followed.

He decided he wasn't going to like this at all.

Gates called sharply.

He ignored him.

Gates groaned and puffed and finally pulled up beside him, matching him stride for stride.

"Listen, pal, just remember—you wouldn't be out now if it wasn't for me. I did the dog-and-pony for you. You think the parole board would have let you out after what you did the last time?"

"So how was I supposed to know they were women?"

The parole officer groaned in exasperation. "You told them they looked like the Three Stooges!"

Hawk shrugged. "One of them was bald and kept saying 'Sointinly.'"

Gates did a slow burn, and Hawk admired the way the officer didn't go for his throat. That was commendable restraint. Trench coat aside, the man did have his points. He didn't, however, much like the storm-cloud look that crossed the man's face a few paces later.

He had a feeling.

He hated having feelings.

When his feelings were right, he usually got into trouble; when his feelings were wrong, he usually got into serious trouble.

Gates tapped his arm. "Remember the guy in the cell next to you, the one who hung himself?"

Hawk did. "Scratchy."

And he didn't like the way Gates smiled.

"And remember that shoe you lost?"

Hawk slowed up, but wouldn't give the man the satisfaction of knowing how he'd suddenly sparked a wave of misgivings. "Yeah. Okay. So now that we've established my photographic memory . . ."

Feelings again.

His muscles were getting tense, his insides were beginning to churn, and this definitely wasn't the way he imagined his first day of freedom. He watched, then, as Gates pulled on a glove that, if anything, was more grimy than his coat, and reached out. From inside the cruiser the driver leaned over the front seat and handed him a shoe.

Gates chuckled humorlessly as he tossed the shoe into the air and caught it. "One phone call. One phone call, and your shoe will become a piece of evidence found in Scratchy's cell. And his suicide'll become murder."

Hawk managed to laugh, but from the sound of his own voice, he didn't think it would fool a stone. "Hey, I don't want you to take this the wrong way, but that's the stupidest fucking thing I've ever heard in my life."

Surprisingly, Gates agreed. "This is the beauty part. It's bullshit." His unwavering grin was unnerving, almost spooky. "But I can make it stick, because I'm the good guy parole officer and you're a bad guy who's about to find out about that thin line."

Hawk didn't say a word.

"So," Gates said, "what's your favorite sport?"

"Baseball, why?"

Gates nodded as if he already knew the answer, and opened the slow-moving cruiser's back door. "Baseball," he growled. Someone handed him a bat.

Hawk moved away warily as Gates hefted the length of wood, sighted along it, took a couple of practice swings, smacked it loudly against his palm.

"Sorry," Hawk said, "I meant Ping-Pong." His face hardened. "Listen, I'd rather go back inside than whore for you, you—" He stopped, slapped his pockets, snapped his fingers. "Oh. I need to borrow ten bucks."

Gates shook his head and came toward him.

Hawk checked the prison wall behind him and saw nothing that would help him climb back over. Above, the only visible guard deliberately turned away.

"Help!" Hawk called weakly. "Police!"

The guard disappeared.

Swell, he thought glumly, just great. They're never around when you need them, and when they are around, they're not here anyway. What the hell is this country coming to, anyway?

Gates grunted as he swung the bat at his head.

Hawk ducked, felt the hardwood brush over the top of his head, and lashed out with one foot, catching the officer's calf with his heel. Gates dropped immediately, then tried to stand up by using his weapon for a crutch. Hawk wasted no time kicking it out of his hand, then snatching it out of the air before it landed in the street.

He stood there with it propped against one shoulder.

Gates flinched, and cowered.

I'd probably get another ten years, Hawk figured, not to mention the murder rap. Maybe life plus, with a couple of weekends off for good behavior. Something told him it would be worth it, just to see if Gates had anything inside him besides hot air; something else, on the other hand, told him that it would be a lot more fun celebrating the turn of the century in his own place, without a few hundred other guys all trying to use the showers at the same time.

It was a close call.

With a sigh of regret, he grabbed the man by the collar and tossed him toward the cruiser, helping him into the backseat with a well-placed kick that produced a satisfying yelp.

Gates righted himself quickly and glared.

Hawk merely stared.

Then the driver stomped on the accelerator and the police car sped away, tires squealing and smoking.

"I don't believe this," he muttered. "I've been out forty seconds—"

And someone fired a gun at the middle of his back.

3

Hawk decided he had just about had enough. Being easygoing had always seen him through most scrapes before, his temper usually held in a tight rein. To let loose was, he'd learned too long ago to remember, only bound to make matters worse, if not downright dangerous. Most people who knew him were aware of this; but there were obviously some left who didn't know that he could be pushed only so far. As a rule, shooting at him, especially in the back, quickly erased the line between a disarming quip and a broken face.

But without a weapon of his own, there wasn't much he could do, especially since that first shot had missed him.

He lay prone on the pavement, anxiously searching for the would-be assailant, hoping there was someplace he could get to before the guy realized he had missed.

Then he saw the Cadillac, and heard it backfire.

His relief was such that he didn't know whether

to laugh at himself for being so skittish or scream at the driver, who pulled the beautifully preserved convertible gunboat to the curb and stepped out. Wearing garish shoes of a style Hawk had last seen on an all-too-successful Forty-second Street pimp.

As he pushed himself up to his knees, the man said, "That's the first thing I did. Smooch the ground and taste the freedom." He laughed. "Sorry I was late, Eddie. Miss anything?"

Hawk stood, brushed himself off, told himself that seeing his friend just about made up for the garbage, and the bat, Gates had tried to ram down his throat.

"As always, Tommy, your timing—and those shoes—are impeccable. God, don't tell me those things are in style now." He looked again and decided not to laugh. Tommy 5-Tone Messina had always been touchy about his ensemble. "Good to see you, man. Been having a lousy day."

Tommy looked at him skeptically. "Lousy day? The man's getting out of prison and he's having a lousy day? What, you missing out on the cell-block water ballet pageant? Believe me, it's overrated."

Hawk started to tell him about Gates and the attempted blackmail and near murder, looked around at the prison still looming behind him, and changed his mind. He wanted away from here; he wanted back with his friends, with real food, with real people.

Not later.

Now.

And it hit him then, for the first time, that he really was free. Out of there. Back in the civilized world. For a second, he almost wept, the emotion

was so strong. To cover himself, he wrapp[e]
arms around Tommy in a silent hug, one tha[t]
everything.

Tommy hugged him back, but his embarrassment, and his pleasure, kept the embrace short.
When they parted, grinning like fools, he said, "So
where's the kiss? No tongue this time, I promise."

Hawk laughed heartily and, as he slipped into
the car, gave his friend's stomach a playful slap.
"Whoa, looks like you've been expanding your—"

"Don't say it, Hawkins," Tommy growled as he
fit himself behind the wheel. "I'm incredibly sen-
sitive about my fucking figure."

"My next word was going to be consciousness,
Tommy. Swear to God. Tubbo."

Tommy said nothing.

Hawk didn't mind. As the Cadillac floated away
from the prison wall and made its way south, he
contented himself with just watching the scenery.
In a curious way it was disappointing, because
nothing seemed to have changed, and it ought to
have after so many years; on the other hand, it was
comforting. A good sign. Despite some of the things
he had heard on the radio, seen on the rec-room TV,
not all that much had changed after all. Fitting
back in ought to be a breeze.

He alternately dozed a little and watched the road
while Tommy chatted about this old buddy and that
one, who married whom, who broke up with whom,
which mayors were assholes and which presidents
were the same, old grudges settled and new ones on
the fire, and always his complaints about how the
economy was going. Down, never up.

No, Hawk decided, nothing had changed.

Halfway there, Tommy gave him a hand puzzle from the glove box, not quite a Rubik's cube, and Hawk beamed. He loved these things. He was good at them, had never yet been stumped, and they allowed him to clear his mind while he worked. Tommy had once called them his Greek worry beads, except he usually didn't have anything to worry about.

This one was no different.

He finished it quickly, with a flourish and proud laugh.

Tommy grumbled.

Hawk held the completed puzzle up. "This is your definition of hard?"

"Show-off. Hey, boss tune: 'Come Fly With Me.' "

"Three minutes fifty-one seconds."

Tommy laughed.

Hawk grinned uncertainly. "What?"

"You crack me up, man."

Hawk wasn't sure what he meant. "What are you laughing at?"

Tommy shrugged. "You crack me up. You still do the puzzles, still know the running times of songs." He shook his head in amused disbelief. "Let me ask you a question: you still think you're the greatest cat burglar who ever lived?"

Hawk stretched, took his time answering. After all, he had had ten years to think about it. Ten years to worry about it. Ten years to wonder.

More miles, then, and more trees, houses, people on the streets as the Cadillac slipped onto the riverside road into Hoboken, Manhattan still gleaming like glass and steel on the eastern horizon.

Nope, he thought as he watched the buildings catch and fire back the sun, nothing changes.

Tommy looked at him.

Okay, Hawk thought, okay.

"No," he said. "Now I'm the laziest cat burglar that ever lived." He puffed his cheeks, blew out slowly. "I'm giving it up. No more stealing."

A silence that lasted for nearly a full mile.

"So hey," Tommy said, "now that you're born again, what do you want to do? Statue of Liberty? Entertain some ladies? Broadway tix? Seduce some women? Play Nintendo? Bone some chicks?"

Hawk gave him a how-crass-you-are look, along with a grin. "What's Nintendo?"

Tommy groaned.

"C'mon, 5-Tone, let's just get to the 5-Tone, okay?" He rubbed the back of his neck. "God, if I don't get some cappuccino soon, I'm going to strangle someone."

Tommy rolled his eyes in feigned disgust. "Oh, man, all this time, you still got a thing for those unmasculine European coffees?" A snort of derision, and he reached into a paper bag set beside him and pulled out a Styrofoam cup. "Who's your buddy?"

After a long moment of not daring to believe it, Hawk took the cup reverently, winked his gratitude, and slipped off the cap. The aroma closed his eyes. "The man knows, the man knows!" He took a slow deep breath, wishing the moment would freeze so that there was nothing else but the silent car, his best friend, and his favorite coffee.

Perfect.

It was perfect.

"So, Mr. Coffee," Tommy said, maneuvering around a van with a deft touch to the wheel, "what went down there outside the prison?"

Hawk shrugged as he brought the cup back to his lips, prolonging the moment, teasing himself. "Not much. Gates just tried to blackmail me into doing a job." Then he yelped when the car braked suddenly and his precious cappuccino flew over his coat, the floor, and the dashboard.

On the other hand, he thought as he licked a few gallant drops from his fingers, nothing lasts forever.

And Tommy's expression was definitely not apologetic. "That doughnut-hole-eating sonofa ... take-it-in-the-ear-for-a-beer rat bastard."

Hawk licked his thumb. "Ah, just the right amount of foam too." He stretched, realized they were close to home, and suddenly looked into the backseat, frowning. "So hey, where's the little guy? Why didn't you bring Little Eddie?"

Tommy didn't answer.

Hawk first thought the man was ready to spring some kind of surprise, and almost smiled until he saw the look in the man's eyes.

He waited.

"Hawk ..." Tommy cleared his throat. "Look, I want you to prepare yourself for some bad news."

And it was.

Without even hearing it, he knew it.

Those damn feelings again.

A cold trace of ice slipped along his spine while, at the same time, something large and hard and coated with acid settled in his stomach. He looked through the windshield and saw nothing.

Nothing lasts.

Tommy pulled a folded newspaper from beneath the bag and tossed it into his lap. "Last night Little Eddie was assassinated."

"What?" He couldn't believe it. A trick of the ears. Too many years blocking out the screams and curses that filled his cell block every night.

"He was rubbed out. Took two shots in the back of the coconut."

Slowly, fingers trembling so hard they scarcely worked, Hawk unfolded the tabloid, scanned the headline, snapped his eyes shut, and waited for an abrupt shudder to pass so that the paper would stop shaking. He swallowed bile. He blinked an abrupt stinging from his eyes. But when he looked again, nothing had changed.

The headline was stark: MONKEY SLAIN IN GANG-LAND HIT!

And beneath it a photograph of a dark street, and on it the all-too-clear chalk outline of a fallen ape.

Worse—an inset picture of Little Eddie, who used to be the healthiest little ape this side of the Mississippi.

Tommy tried to say something, but Hawk waved him silent with a slash of his hand. Then he took several deep breaths trying to stop the scream that bubbled in his throat.

He didn't scream.

He wailed.

He wept.

He finally descended into a morose slump that didn't improve when Tommy finally pulled up in front of the 5-Tone Bar. When he opened the door, it was with a singular lack of enthusiasm; when he glanced at the Empire State Building across the river to the east, it was without his usual welcoming wave; when he reached for the door, Tommy touched his arm.

"He was more than just a monkey, you know, he was a true friend."

Hawk sighed. "He was like a son to me."

"He was like a nephew to me," Tommy said.

Hawk nodded, then rolled his shoulders, straightened his back. "Just get me in the bar. It's the one thing that will never—"

He stepped inside.

He whispered hoarsely, "—change."

Tommy stayed behind him, so he couldn't run back out.

It was an easy thing to conclude that someone had shot him after all, and that he'd been immediately, without benefit of jury trial, sent directly to Hell, do not pass Go, do not change your clothes, it won't matter, they'll be fried off in a few minutes.

Ten years ago, the 5-Tone had been an ordinary, personable Jersey watering hole. The customers were friendly, the bartender could run a dozen tabs with half his brain tied behind his back, and while it wasn't exactly making him or Tommy rich, it paid the bills and gave him more hours of solid pleasure than anyplace else he'd ever known.

He gaped.

He looked at Tommy.

He looked back at the bar.

He had been warned that Hoboken was on the fast road to gentrification, but this, he thought, was ridiculous to the point of lunacy.

Art deco in every conceivable spot that wasn't

drifting with ferns, plastic, and neon, insufferably
loud music he couldn't identify and didn't much
care to, lighting that would make a blind man feel
at home . . . and not a single hard hat or cloth cap
or denim jacket in sight.

He wasn't sure, but he thought he gasped.

He knew he had to rub his eyes when, as he made
his stunned way toward the bar itself, he saw a
young couple actually toast each other with wine
coolers; he also knew that bull's-eyes would never
be the same when he spotted a pair of young men,
in suits for God's sake, high-five each other at the
dart board.

He staggered.

Tommy grabbed his arm, immediately let it go.
"I didn't know how to tell you," he said nervously.
"A couple brokers stopped in for Stoley Spritzers
one night. Next thing I know *Fast Track Digest*
votes us Watering Hole of the Month." His laugh
was nervous as well. "Now I'm shopping for aqua-
salmon wallpaper."

I'm not in New Jersey, Hawk thought; aliens
have abducted me and I'm somewhere on Mars.

Jesus!

"I read about these people in *Newsweek*. I—" He
checked the crowd again, wincing when a particularly loud blast of music threatened to bring down
the ceiling. "Where are all the regulars? Crazy Jeff
Cava, the Todd sisters, Indian Joe?" He swallowed
heavily. "Where's Ed Kranepool's autograph? Jesus, you took down Captain Bob's steering wheel?"

Forget Mars, he thought, I'm in freaking Won-
derland.

"All gone," Tommy answered. "But look on the

bright side, Hawk. Half the joint is yours." He lifted the bar's flap. "Hey, Blackjack, get my irritable partner here a cappuccino. I gotta go be a boss."

Hawk took an empty stool and, doing his best not to scream, picked up a menu. Glanced at it. Looked around for Tommy. "This is pizza? Reindeer goat cheese? Hey, I admit I've been known to go wild in my time and order Canadian bacon but . . ."

No one listened.

He dropped the menu and decided that there was nothing he could do now, even if he wanted to. Watch and observe, instead, and maybe, with luck, all these yuppies will find someplace else to ruin and things will get normal again.

He took a cigarette from his pocket and lit it, inhaled, and glanced around just in time to look into the tortoiseshell face of the man beside him.

The man pointed at a large button pinned to his lapel. "Can you read . . . smoker?"

Hawk did: YES, I MIND IF YOU SMOKE.

Hawk shook his head in disappointment. "You know, I thought this was a country where you could do any stupid thing you wanted—drive to work naked, spank a chiropractor, make love to a VCR. Maybe that's why I became a random collector of kneecaps."

Hawk counted the seconds it took for the jerk to realize he just may not be kidding.

Four.

"Hey, it's okay, big guy. Smoke all you want. Have mine—"

Hawk did his best not to laugh when the man fumbled an open pack of cigarettes from his jacket, tossed it on the bar, and fled.

Lord, he thought, Lord.

Then Tommy called him, he turned and deftly snared a sliding cup-and-saucer in one hand. He smiled at the cappuccino offering, lifted the cup, and swiveled around to continue his watch-and-observe assessment of what used to be one hell of a neighborhood bar. He brought the cup to his lips, smiled again when he remembered what happened the last time he'd tried to drink, and prepared himself for a treat.

And thought, barely blinking, why not? when someone shot the cup from his hand.

4

This shooting business, thought Hawk, is getting to be a habit.

Even worse: the way things were going, Sing Sing was beginning to look like home sweet home.

This is not, he thought further, a very good sign. The nuns who had raised him would probably have a fit.

As he brushed the coffee from his jacket and dropped the shattered remains of the cup on the bar, he checked the room again. Calmly. Evidently, by all appearances, no one had heard or seen anything, which explained why there wasn't a lot of screaming and yelling and running in panic for the exits. Then, at a far corner table tucked away from most of the customers, he spotted what had to be the world's most obvious thug, Antony Mario, smiling at him as he thrust a silencer-adjusted revolver into his sharkskin trousers. Beside him, still seated and eating as if nothing untoward had happened, was his older brother, Cesar. Another thug, to be sure, but one who at least knew how to dress himself.

Cesar beckoned him with a finger.

Hawk sneered and looked away.

When he looked back, the man beckoned a second time, impatiently.

There was a great, close to overwhelming temptation to continue ignoring him, to make him get his unlawfully fat butt out of his chair and come over here, but the aroma of his precious, untasted coffee lingered on his jacket and hands, and he decided that the Mario brothers had just about erased the line. Messing with him was one thing; messing with his cappuccino was something else again.

He rolled his shoulders to shake off the tension and decided what the hell, maybe he could rent them to breathe on the damn ferns and kill them.

Smiling and nodding to the oblivious customers he passed, he took his time making his way to the table, reminding himself with every step that he was still only a few glorious hours out of prison and had no plans of going back anytime soon.

Be cool; that was the key.

"Nice shot, Antony," he congratulated when he reached the mobsters' table, not failing to note the stone-faced bodyguards flanking the man's brother.

"Fuck you, Eddie," the man answered smugly.

Screw the line, Hawk decided, life's too short and so is this jerk.

Before anyone could move, he slugged the man square on his blunt jaw, setting him into his chair, nearly toppling it backward. One of the bodyguards whipped out a knife, but as Hawk turned to meet it, Cesar stayed the man with a gesture.

A moment.

The bodyguard retreated.

Hawk grinned. "Cesar Mario, Antony Mario, when did the circus get in?" His voice hardened. "And who killed my monkey?"

Hastily, Cesar pushed aside his platter of steaming pasta and lifted his palms and napkin to fend off the anger. He dabbed his lips, sniffed, carefully folded the napkin back on the table, and realigned his silverware. "Let's clear some air here," he said calmly. "My hand to God, we didn't whack Little Eddie, okay? I never had anything against the kooky chimp. I actually found him . . . endearing."

"Oh, sure," Hawk replied, not bothering to temper his disbelief. He leaned over the table without actually moving. "Facedown. Two endearing shots to the back of his endeared head. That's your trademark, Cesar. Your mark. What did Little Eddie ever do to—"

Antony sneered. "So some little banana eater got iced. What's the big—"

He blanched when Hawk took a sudden step toward him, not relaxing at all when Cesar waved his hands as if to clear the air and calm them down. "Sit." He looked at Hawk. "So why won't you do the auction house?"

Hawk didn't let his surprise show, but he began to wonder how many players were trying to play this game. It was beginning to get on his nerves.

Cesar asked him again.

Hawk sighed. "Auction houses are very popular this season." No one said anything. He shrugged.

"Call me superstitious, but I don't like to commit a crime less than twenty-four hours after getting out of prison."

Some raucous cheering from the dart board made him wince; the appearance of a small black bag on the table made him feel abruptly, and uncomfortably, weary. He let himself down into a chair by stages, like an old man, not taking his gaze from the gangster's face.

Television monitors had been placed on black wrought-iron shelves high on the walls around the 5-Tone. He glanced up at the nearest one, didn't recognize the program except that it was a game show, looked away, and wondered where Tommy had been hiding during all this. It wasn't like him.

On the other hand, neither were the stupid ferns.

Cesar shoveled some food into his mouth and pushed it into one cheek, waved a fork over his pasta, rolled a meatball to one side, and poked at it several times to be sure Hawk was paying attention. He swallowed with a mouthful of wine. "It's very simple. There's a safe on the seventh floor. From this safe you take out a thingie and put it in this thingie—"

"Or you cut off my thingie." Hawk didn't smile. "Directions even your brother would understand."

Antony bridled. "Yeah. Directions even I could understand."

Cesar glared at him. "Silence."

Hawk resisted the temptation to grin. While this wasn't even remotely what he wanted to do with the rest of his life, he couldn't help but wonder just what was going on here. First there was that slime-ball Gates, now the local mafioso. He couldn't quite put his finger on it, but there was something wrong in the state of New Jersey.

Something very wrong.

Cesar nodded toward the bag, swallowed another mouthful of his dinner. "Hawk, you're the best. No one but you can do it." He leaned back and folded his hands in his lap, his expression brooking no more nonsense from either him or his brother. "So don't give me a line of bullshit about how you really want to go straight, open a hardware store and sell spatulas."

One of his feelings began screaming in his ear.

Very wrong indeed.

It didn't take him longer than half a second to decide that he wanted no part of whatever this thug was selling. When slime started working with slime, not even a boiling shower was going to keep you clean. And clean, especially now, was exactly how he intended to stay.

Cesar waited patiently, not smiling, only watching.

Hawk waited for him to swallow again. "You know what, Cesar? If the Mario brothers weren't Jersey's third-largest crime family, I'd say kiss my ass. But," he added quickly, "considering your status, I'll just say slurp my butt."

He tensed then when Antony yanked the gun out again, and tried to decide if he could get across the table before the idiot either shot him, or shot himself in the foot and sued them out of business. Either way, even the new breed of customers weren't going to be able to miss this one, and that meant the police, and that meant—

Tommy arrived just as Antony had turned the

barrel toward his chest. In his hand was a bottle expertly wrapped in a white towel. "Have you lovely folks tried our house wine? I think you'll enjoy—"

Hawk didn't relax; he could see that the mobster wasn't buying the interruption. A quick glance at Cesar, who hadn't moved an inch.

"Beat it, Tommy," Antony said, voice low and toneless, "no dinosaurs allowed."

Messina cheerfully tossed the towel aside and split the bottle over Antony's head, and just as cheerfully eased away from the splash with his hands pulled to his chest. "It's oh-so-smooth, but not too precocious."

Hawk didn't move.

Antony, disbelief on his features, fluttered his eyes closed and began to sag toward the table.

Cesar had had enough. Slapping his napkin to the table, he stood, took a deep breath, and scowled. "Forget Gates and your little shoe," he spat quietly. "You don't do the job and *we'll* put you on trial. And believe me, there won't be a bailiff in the room."

With an angry, impatient chopping gesture, he ordered his men to their feet and led them from the room, two of them half carrying, half dragging a dazed Antony between them. When they were gone, Hawk decided it was all right to breathe, and thanked Tommy for the help with a wink and a nod. It was time, he thought, for something to drink. Not cappuccino, however; that had become a rather high-risk move.

He eased back through the crowd, marveling again at the redecoration, trying to figure out just how Tommy could have done so little with so much, when one of the people standing at the bar turned around.

It was Gates.

Hawk stopped.

The parole officer noted him with a humorless wave and walked out without looking back.

Hawk and Messina exchanged glances.

Tommy looked back.

Don't, Hawk ordered himself, do not look.

The music quieted for a moment.

Do not look.

He looked.

Oh, shit, he thought.

On the table, in the middle, was the small black bag.

5

The back room of the 5-Tone was a combination office and storeroom, and it was here, that night, that Hawk found all the stuff Tommy had taken down from the walls when the yuppie invasion began. It was . . . depressing.

He wandered around the tables, the piles of junk, puffed his cheeks and sighed at the filing cabinets they had always swore they'd use for their records but never had. Any flat surface was good enough.

He wandered.

He sighed.

He watched Tommy standing over the floor plans of the Rutherford Auction House.

He reminded himself, three or four hundred times at last count, that he was going straight.

" 'Mack the Knife,' " Tommy said.

"Three-oh-five."

Absently. It was automatic. All automatic.

" 'I Only Have Eyes for You.' "

He grinned. "Why, Tommy, I didn't know you cared. Three minutes thirty-nine seconds."

In a pile in a corner he found a steering wheel, and the sight of it wrenched his heart.

" 'Xanadu,' " Tommy said.

Hawk picked the wheel up and showed it to him. "Three-thirty, and how could you take this down? Don't you remember the night Captain Bob came in, out of his mind? Nobody could figure out where he got this thing."

Tommy didn't answer. He jabbed a finger at a photograph of a safe. "Nasty little safe on the seventh floor. Simpson seventy-one."

Hawk put the wheel down and stood over the table, looked at the picture, shook his head. "Last time I played the game, Simpson only made a forty."

Messina shrugged. "Just means it'll take you an extra thirty-one seconds to figure it out."

Hawk groaned silently and walked away, looked at the ceiling, looked back at his friend. "I'm not worried about the safe. What about the house guards? You know any of them? What about the electronic surveillance equipment?"

Tommy laughed, pointed a finger-gun at him. "I got a plan."

"Oh. Oh, you got a plan."

"Yeah," Messina said, insulted. "Yeah, I got a great plan."

Hawk shook his head. "What the hell am I doing? I just got out of jail and I'm robbing some auction house, stealing some *vercachte* horse with you." His hands raised to the ceiling, fell to his sides wearily. "Man, I should be going out, buying the *Daily*

News, going through the want ads looking for a job selling spatulas."

He felt lousy.

He felt worse than lousy.

He felt as if he wanted to cry, scream, take somebody's head and put it through a wall.

Tommy hurried over to him, grabbed his hands. "Eddie, Eddie, I'm sorry, man. I'm movin' too fast. I'm putting out a fire with kerosene." Then he stepped away, grinning.

Hawk looked down; his hands were pinned with Chinese thumbcuffs. "What is this?"

"That's five seconds," Tommy said, grinning. "My record's eighteen."

Hawk was not amused. The thumbcuffs reminded him of the nuns. He yanked the cuffs off effortlessly and threw them across the room, knocking a lamp over, making Tommy jump back. "You think this is funny?" He swallowed, trying to keep his voice from going through the roof. "This is your idea of a joke?" He stalked across the room, determined to tell the Mario brothers and Gates to take a flying leap.

"Can't . . . can't we just not do it?"

Stupid question.

He was caught; he knew it.

Neither Gates nor the Mafia were the sort to take "Sorry, boys, I have a splitting headache" as an excuse. And he did not, absolutely did not want to spend one more day behind bars.

Shit.

His shoulders slumped. "How many seconds?" he asked softly.

"How many seconds what?"

"On the cuffs."

"Well . . . not counting the bitching and whining, I'll be nice and say eight."

Swell, Hawk thought, big . . . deal.

Tommy pushed the floor plans around, looked up. "You think you still got it?"

It took a while before Hawk finally nodded. "Yeah. That's what I'm afraid of." He almost laughed then at the absurdity of it all. "You know," he said, "I ain't never going to get rehabilitated this way."

A thought that occurred to him at least five times a minute for the rest of the day, and especially when they entered the spa next door to Rutherford's that night. On the other hand, he had to admit that there was nothing like a good heist and the threat of spending the rest of his life behind bars—or getting aced by Antony Mario—to get the old competitive juices flowing, the old gears back into shape, the old instincts working, the old bullshit he always used to justify his thievery.

And the curiosity, he told himself, don't forget the curiosity. Something's wrong, remember? You want to find out what's really going on here.

Something else reminded him what the cat had learned about curiosity, and he told himself to shut up and deal. This was no time to be having second thoughts, especially when he'd already worked his way through the fifth and the sixth ones several hours ago.

He checked the cut of his maintenance uniform, nodded to Tommy, and they pushed through the door to the pool together, nearly giving an ancient janitor his fatal heart attack.

"Hey, what are you guys doing here? I thought you came on Thursdays."

"Emergency," Tommy explained briskly. "Pool's infested with—"

Hawk waited, trying not to breathe in the strong smell of chlorine.

"Infested with . . ." Tommy glanced at him, pleading for help.

"Sea monkeys."

The janitor's eyes widened. "Sea monkeys?"

Tommy shook his head as if not believing it himself. "Happens all the time, man. Kids order them from the back of comic books."

"Moms flush 'em down the toilets," Hawk added solemnly, and stifled a giveaway laugh that nearly choked him when Tommy looked around and clucked his tongue.

"You got a gas mask?" Messina asked the old man.

The janitor swallowed. "No. Why?"

"You may want to get out of here," Hawk suggested then. "We're going to be spraying some toxic . . . uh . . ."

"Stuff," Tommy said.

Hawk nodded emphatically. "Stuff."

The janitor, who had clearly decided these boys had lost more than a few bricks of their load, looked from one to the other and sighed in resignation. "Sure," he grumbled, grabbing his mop and shambling away. "Whatever. I'm leaving anyway. It's the end of my shift."

They smiled and nodded at the muttering custodian until Hawk thought his head would fall off. The moment they were alone, however, they wasted no time grabbing what they needed—Tommy snaring a pair of life preservers from poolside while Hawk gathered in the floating lane dividers. Then they hustled through the rear exit and up the staircase to the roof, where Hawk clipped the dividers together into a single strand while Tommy lashed a preserver at either end.

Hawk watched then as Tommy hurried to the edge and shaded his eyes. There was a small terrace on the other side, and below it a ledge from which protruded an exposed, capped pipe. When it was obvious there was nothing on the terrace to use for an anchor, he gauged the distance, drew back his arm, and flung one of the preservers at the pipe, neatly hooking it the first time. When the line was pulled taut, the anchor tested to be sure it wouldn't pull loose, he hooked the other end over a pipe on the roof and tightened the knot.

Quietly.

Swiftly.

Out of their uniforms, revealing black from throat to ripple-soled shoes.

If I were a bird, Hawk thought as he slipped over the edge and started a hand-over-hand journey to the other side, I wouldn't have to do this crap. On the other hand, if I were a bird, I wouldn't need the damn money.

Tommy puffed behind him. "Hey, Hawk, look down. Look down, buddy. Come on, your shoe's untied."

Hawk laughed instead of looking. It was one

thing to be dangling over a zillion-foot drop; it was something else again to actually have to look at it.

"Shut up," he said. "Whoa, did you say this thing only holds nine hundred pounds?"

"Cold," Tommy muttered. "That's cold, Hawkins."

Hawk couldn't resist: "Hey, somebody's down there stealing your Caddy, look."

Messina's voice grew a little high-pitched and desperate. "Cut that shit, huh? You know I can't look down. It makes my balls tingle."

Hawk cut it. He knew about Tommy's phobia, knew he shouldn't kid about it, but there were times, like now, when he needed to take his mind off falling to his death. The rope sagged, swayed when a gust of wind tunneled through the alley, and he was sure that a crowd was already forming on the sidewalk, watching him, taking his picture, calling the local news stations so they, and he, could get on TV.

Messina cursed.

Hawk concentrated on swinging his feet up to the ledge, not waiting to rest until he was flat up against the wall, hugging it and feeling the sweat begin to gather and run down the middle of his back. It was cold. His heart worked overtime. His legs had begun to protest maltreatment. Then Tommy joined him a second later and, as soon as he was steady, grabbed the life preserver and flung it back to the health spa roof.

Hawk couldn't believe his eyes. "What's the matter with you?"

"Covers our tracks," the man explained easily. "We'll leave through the basement."

"Well, we don't have any choice, do we?"

"What?"

Hawk didn't think this was the time to argue, or to explain that he was not pleased that this part of the plan hadn't been explained to him first. Instead, he scrambled up and over the terrace wall and stood there, hands on his hips, waiting for his nerves and his pulse to calm down. A lot of time had passed since last he'd tried something like that, and despite the workouts in the prison gym, the jogging around the yard, he was still ten years older. Frighteningly, those spatulas were beginning to look awfully good.

Tommy leapt easily to the terrace and brandished an old-fashioned glass-cutter he used to point at the window on the other side. A quick check to be sure they were alone, and he moved there without a sound, measured the glass with one eye half-closed, and began to cut.

"This'll get us into the office."

Hawk stared pointedly at the man's stomach. "Well, you'd better cut a bigger hole than that, then."

"Don't worry, you fuck, I'm wearing my girdle."

Less than thirty seconds, and a large glass hole eased into his hands. Carefully he placed it on the terrace and, before Hawk could think of anything else to say, wriggled through to the other side.

You can leave now, Eddie, he suggested, it's still not too late.

Tommy waved at him impatiently.

Leave now, go to Iowa or someplace, work the rest of your life for charity or something.

Tommy rapped on the window.

Man's always nagging, he thought, and slipped easily inside, and found himself in a claustrophobic men's room that hadn't been cleaned in at least a century. Tommy ducked through the door, and he followed, exiting into a long, quiet hall. A faint, intermittent whirring sound made him look up, and he tapped Messina's shoulder, pointing to a security camera bracketed to the wall just above their heads.

"Auction room's through that door down there," he whispered.

Tommy shook his head. "We got another stop first."

The moment the lens swiveled away from them, they scuttled swiftly along the wall to a door marked POWER, which Hawk was not thrilled to note was right next to the guard station; and that place was open.

And occupied.

Two guards were at the kind of security desk Hawk had seen only in movies—cameras, monitors, microphones, and a dozen gadgets he couldn't identify. What he did see, however, was that each of the screens clearly covered most of the building, including the room where the Simpson 71 was.

One of the guards flipped through a large telephone book. "Wong's in the book," he told his partner.

"Hell of a lot of Wong numbers," the other man answered.

Hawk checked the door impatiently; it was locked.

"Is this it?" he whispered.

Tommy nodded. "Yeah."

"You got a key?"

"Nope." And he bent over to work on picking the lock.

"Just checking." He looked over at the guard station; the two men were laughing quietly. "Tommy."

Impatiently: "What?"

"Are the Mets playing tonight?"

Tommy didn't look up. "They're playing at Shea."

Hawk sighed at the injustice of the world. "Figures. I got to be robbing an auction house."

"Since when were you a Mets fan?"

"I've always been a Mets fan."

Tommy didn't answer; the tumblers turned, and they slipped noiselessly inside, closed the door behind them, and he stared at the VCRs ranged on a shelf. Their wires dangled to the floor and through the wall to, he realized, the monitors on the other side. Messina pointed at the machines, all of them whirring softly, LED displays blinking the time and marking off the length of tape that wound through them. "They record everything, I mean everything their video surveillance takes in."

Swell, Hawk thought, they see everything, they record everything. They know everything that's going on. This was a lousy time to be told he was going to have to be a damn ghost to pull this job off.

Tommy pointed again, just to be sure Hawk understood.

Hawk didn't like the implication.

"Yes, Master Thief, I can see that, okay? So. You said something about a plan?"

6

Hawk looked in bewilderment at the VCRs, the wires, the VCRs, the wires, and decided that he ought to find a new profession, and he'd better do it fast. Too much new technology had come into the world while he'd been out of it, and the very sight of it made his head begin to ache.

This, he thought, was not going to be a happy time.

Tommy, meanwhile, was busily pushing all the rewind buttons on the machines. He glanced over his shoulder and said, "Am I boring you, smart-ass?" A quick gesture to direct Hawk's attention back to the job at hand. "A little rewind, see, and rewire action here, and the guards are going to be watching a rerun and miss out on our exciting episode."

Hawk thought a moment.

Hawk smiled.

Maybe, he thought, high tech wasn't so bad after all.

* * *

Stan Gardner didn't mind being a guard. It wasn't the most exciting job in the world, but that's one of the reasons why he liked it. Too much excitement meant work was involved, and work was not at the top of his list of all-time fun ways to pass the time.

Tonight, for example, was perfect—quiet, no auction personnel around, the guys keeping out of his face, and a chance now to take a quick snooze before he had to check in. He figured the owners wouldn't mind; it wasn't like they were paying a fortune to him to protect their stupid paintings and statues, most of which he wouldn't let within ten miles of his home. Most of it was crap. He didn't know much about art, but he definitely knew crap, and this shit was it.

Sometimes it made him wonder. Just wonder.

He wandered through the seventh-floor auditorium, footsteps echoing, breath a little loud. Chairs were scattered across the floorboards, a huge polisher still plugged in and parked in the center. No bad guys here, he thought with a chuckle, and made his way to the large stage at the back, and to a blue chair in the rear, set beneath a painting of children playing on a swing. It was an ordinary-size chair, but Stan wasn't, so it took a bit of wriggling and a couple of grunts before he was able to make himself comfortable.

Nice, he decided.

He glanced around the auditorium one more time, sighed contentedly, and tipped the chair back, ready for a quick forty winks before the guys realized he was gone.

* * *

The guys knew he was gone.

At the guard station, Jerry watched the auditorium monitor and grinned as he saw Big Stan pick the place for his nightly nap. He waited until Stan's eyes were closed, then picked up his walkie-talkie and clicked the button a few times, nudging his partner.

"Hey, Mac, check out Big Stan."

Mac squinted at the screen and laughed, and shook his head as Jerry pressed the transmit button, choked back a giggle, and said loudly, "Big Stan!"

It was like watching their own private television show, without the damn commercials.

Stan snorted in surprise, kicked out, flailed his arms, and the chair, in excruciating slow motion, collapsed and splintered around him.

Adrenaline began to rush and peak, bringing Hawk almost up on his toes. His senses heightened, his muscles jumped, he could hear the guards laughing at something out at the station. His anger at the Mario brothers faded to insignificance; his fervent desire to be somewhere else faded as well. It was happening, he couldn't do anything about it, so he might as well let go and let the flow take him. As long as he kept his head straight, as long as he wasn't too rusty, he ought to be able to get out of this without a scratch, and without Gates hanging on to him for the rest of his life.

Tommy popped the last of last Monday's tapes

• 49 •

into the last machine and began checking the wiring at the back, hands in an efficient, amazing blur.

"You've got about five minutes and change."

Timing.

Hawk loved it. "Okay. 'Swinging on a Star.' "

Messina grimaced. "You know, they invented something while you were inside. It's called a watch."

Hawk grinned and inched open the door. A quick check of the corridor, and he began to sing under his breath the song Swinging on a Star.

To keep the synchronization intact, Tommy couldn't argue. He continued with the next line of the song while hurrying to a circuit box on the wall near the door. The lid opened easily. A fast read of the switches and he yanked two of them down simultaneously.

The lights went out.

The monitoring station went blank.

Hawk instantly slipped out of the room and closed the door behind him, sprinted down the hall as he heard one of the guards curse and another one say, "Hell-o. Better check the power room, Mac."

Hawk never faltered, singing the song to keep his timing perfect.

Tommy, working mostly by touch and a strong, well-defined sense of not wanting to get his little Italian ass caught, swiftly reattached the machines. In virtually the same movement, he slapped all the play buttons.

He didn't hesitate, didn't panic when he heard a guard pause outside the door, noisily fumbling through his set of keys and muttering to himself. He slammed the power circuit switches back into position, and snapped his fingers, whistled silently when the lights returned.

The guard grunted.

Tommy puffed his cheeks in relief, checked the VCRs one last time, and cat-walked silently to the door, smiling as he heard the guard grumble back toward his post. Holding his breath then, he opened the door a crack and put his ear to it, waiting for his chance to slip out and head for the auditorium. He heard footsteps approaching the station. Gingerly, he poked his head out far enough to see down the hall. And to spot a large guard lumber toward the consoles, dropping bits of what looked like a chair in his wake.

"Very funny," the big guard said.

Tommy had no idea what the man was talking about, and he didn't much care. What was important was what they would see when they looked at the screens—nothing.

Nothing but a very peaceful, and very empty, auditorium.

Hawk skid-ran into the auditorium and, after a quick check of a piece of paper grabbed from his pocket, headed straight for the stage.

Kicking aside some puzzling debris, he snatched the painting off the wall and grinned at the safe revealed behind it. No imagination, he thought, pulling a Walkman from one of his pockets; don't these guys ever watch movies? He attached a suction cup to the safe, plugged it into the Walkman, and readied himself.

He almost panicked, but faked the words of his song to keep the timing right. There was no room for error. Screwup meant lockup.

Tommy raced down the hall toward a waiting freight elevator, singing quietly as he went. He quickly continued his way to the auditorium.

In the meantime, Hawk rotated the safe dial notch by notch, shuddered when the clicks were loud enough to turn his brain to mush, and quickly thumbed down the volume. A moment later he heard a very satisfying clunk.

Bingo, he thought. Lord, Lord, the man ain't lost the touch.

Mac sipped his coffee, grimaced at the plastic taste, and sipped again.

And didn't swallow.

A brief perplexed frown worked his brow. He looked more closely at the seventh screen on the bank before him. Something was wrong there. Maybe. Or maybe he was just tired, listening to Big Stan bellyache all night, listening to Jerry complain about all his girlfriends—maybe he was shutting down his brain without realizing it.

He looked at the screen again.

Then he looked at the floor.

Now he knew he was no Einstein, which was why he had this damn job in the first place, but he also knew how to add two and two and not end up with eighty-seven.

"Uh, Jerry."

Jerry grunted.

"Jerry, I'm looking at the seventh floor and ... I don't know how to say this, but I see the blue chair."

Jerry scowled. "What the ..." He scanned the monitors and muttered a curse to himself. "You think that's weird, check out screen two."

Mac looked.

He blinked.

He didn't like the thought that began to niggle the edges of his mind.

There he was on screen two, with Jerry, walking down a hall as they each popped a can of beer.

He stared, then looked to the empty cans sitting atop the console.

It didn't take him long: "Somebody rewired the recorders!"

With a flourish, Hawk tossed his equipment aside and pulled open the safe.

Beautiful, he thought, just beautiful.

A moment's admiration for a job well done, and he reached in, pulling out an exquisite clay equestrian statue. Behind him, Tommy also swelled with pride.

As Hawk put the statue carefully in the bag, they laughed, thumbs-up at each other, and decided there was nothing wrong with finishing the song together; after all they were a team. After all, they were already on a stage. Exuberantly they sang the last few lines of the song, finishing with a flourish.

Yes, Hawk thought, it just doesn't get much better.

Big Stan muttered grumpily as he reconnected the wires of the seventh VCR, fingers fumbling with the thin wires. This wasn't part of his job. This was—

Suddenly, from out at the station, he heard Jerry yell, "Shit, let's roll!"

Time's up, Hawk realized as he hurried to clean up, time's up.

He grabbed the painting and deftly hooked it back onto the wall.

Time's up.

He saw the children, playing on the swing.

He stopped.

Tommy pounded his shoulder. "Come on! The song's over."

Hawk shook his head. "What am I doing here? I never wanted to do this. I wanted to play it straight."

Tommy sounded close to panic. "C'mon, I *said* the song's over."

Hawk sighed, and looked at his friend. "I wouldn't tape a Mets game without the express written consent of major league baseball."

He had no time to say anything else.

The auditorium doors slammed open with an explosive crash, and the two station guards swept into the room.

"Damn, the song was over," Tommy said flatly. "You couldn't have waited to see a psychiatrist. No, you had to—" He grabbed the nearest chair and flung it end over end at the floor polisher. It tipped forward on its broad base, yanking its cord up high enough to trip the onrushing guards onto their stomachs.

"Safe at third," Hawk called with a laugh, then

immediately ran straight at them before they had a chance to regain their feet. A quick flurry, and they yowled when they realized he had slipped them into Tommy's thumbcuffs. Then he ducked away from their flailing arms.

"The back way," he called to Tommy.

The rear door slammed open, and Big Stan puffed his way into the room.

"Keep those ideas coming," Tommy said.

Hawk paid him no heed. Though Stan didn't look all that agile or bright, he was definitely large enough to cause serious damage should he get one of those massive hands around his neck. He whipped around and charged for the front, Tommy right behind him. They dodged the stumbling guards still enmeshed in the thumbcuffs and raced into the hall. He didn't bother to look back; he could hear that third guard thundering along like an enraged hippo.

A painting, he thought as he charged for the men's room and their escape; I had to stop for a lousy painting. I'm getting soft. And as he flung himself around the corner, skidding, caroming lightly off the opposite wall, he realized that what he'd told Tommy had been right on the money—he really didn't want to do this.

Choices, however, had been reduced to nothing.

Bring the damn horse to Mario, take a bow, and get back to his life.

Nothing to it.

And easier said than done when he squirmed through the hole in the window and stood on the terrace, the chilled night air colder because of the sweat that had broken out on his face. He helped

Tommy through and sprinted to the edge, preparing himself for the next move. No haste now, no matter what. One step at a time. First, the climb across to the roof; then a quick race down the stairs before those other guards extracted themselves—or learned damn quick how to be Siamese; then a leap into Tommy's Caddy; then . . . then . . .

He looked down at the pipe.

Tommy looked down at the pipe.

They both looked at the rope coiled on the health spa roof across the alley.

"I cannot tell you how happy I am," Hawk said, "that we covered our tracks."

Tommy looked hurt. "Hey, I'm not as fat as that guard, am I?"

Hawk glanced at the window. "Of course not, man, you're a reed. Look."

Big Stan had somehow managed to wedge himself into the gap, which might have made them laugh had it not been for the gun in the hand that had not, unfortunately, been caught as well.

Stan saw them.

He fired.

Hawk let his instincts take over, and take him over the terrace wall and onto the ledge, Tommy close behind. Since there was no way across the alley without a miraculous growth of wings, he edged as best he could toward the auction building's front, wincing when he heard a dull thud above him that suggested all too strongly for his nerves that the guard had finally dumped himself onto the terrace.

He looked down, and groaned.

The only thing between him and the sidewalk was the auction house's large canopy.

Tommy followed his gaze and tried to push himself into the stone.

"Hang on, Slim Jim," Hawk told him. "Hang on."

He heard the guard scrambling across the terrace.

"I have a bad feeling," they told each other.

Hawk swallowed. "I can't even swim."

"Hell," Tommy said, "the fall'll probably kill you."

No way, Hawk thought, no way in hell. There had to be another out. He had the name, but he sure as hell didn't have the feathers.

A shot, and a piece of masonry showered over their heads.

Hawk looked back and saw the guard leaning over the terrace wall, steadying his gun with both hands.

He wasn't about to miss again.

Damn, he thought.

He jumped.

7

It wasn't the fall so much that Hawk minded, although he did manage a desperate prayer to every god and goddess in the known universe on the way down, and quite a few that he made up along the way.

And it wasn't landing cleanly on the awning and nearly bouncing off on his head that made him wish Big Stan had put him out of his misery.

Nor, now that he thought about it, was it the maniacal way Tommy drove away from the auction house, even if he did nearly wrap them both around a telephone pole, a parking sign, and a pushcart.

No.

What really ticked him off was Gates's apartment.

It was, he thought as he dropped heavily into a La-Z-Boy large enough to land several jet fighters and a blimp, the man's blatant offense to good decorating taste, or even halfway decent taste of any kind.

Appalling was about the kindest word he could think of.

The multicolored carpet was shaggy enough, and thick and high and encrusted enough, to remind him of a tropical jungle in serious need of preservation; the peeling walls were of a color that he was fairly positive hadn't yet been invented—the man actually had the nerve to feature a large framed print of half a dozen dogs playing draw poker around a green-felt table; and beside a flickering stereo that was barely able to play one note at a time was a chipped and cheap punch bowl filled with a suspicious red liquid that, given half a chance, would probably start bubbling.

He went through all that—and nearly got shot and squashed in the process—to end up . . . here.

Life, he thought, has a lot of explaining to do.

Gates himself, in an open-neck, blinding Hawaiian shirt and shorts exposing bandy legs pale as a fish's belly, took the canvas bag from his hands and toasted him with a tumbler of that foul red stuff.

"Hudson Hawk," he said expansively, and a little late, "gets the chair of honor. How about a Gates-arita? I used real hot dogs."

Hawk refused with a strained smile. "I bet you were the bartender at Jonestown, right?"

A lamp flashed on in the corner, and Hawk nodded to Cesar Mario. Antony stood beside him, gamely sipping a glass of Gates's concoction.

"Good job," Cesar acknowledged grudgingly. "Not pretty, but good."

Hawk shrugged. "Ah, the Mafia, the cops—do I know how to party or what?"

Gates, meanwhile, unzipped the bag and, after

some rooting around inside, pulled out the equestrian model and stared at it in surprise, turned it over, held it up to the light. "All this trouble for a horsey? I may not know art, but I know what I like."

Hawk glanced at the dogs-and-poker-game on the wall. "You certainly do."

The parole officer turned to Cesar. "So when's that Sebastian Cabot Buckingham Palace–looking butlerhead, Alfred, getting here?"

Hawk frowned, and was about to ask a question when he was interrupted by a very British voice: "Any minute now, dear Mr. Gates."

He twisted around, not really wanting to know who else had suddenly become involved; it was hard enough keeping track of them already. What he saw was a man who had obviously been born with white gloves and a butler's uniform already on. As he glided deeper into the room, Hawk noticed his expression cloud over briefly when he glanced down at a magazine on a coffee table. Hawk checked himself and saw a cover photograph of a tycoon type, a woman, and a small dog. The caption announced *Mayflower Power*, which meant absolutely nothing to him.

"Oh," Gates said. "Sorry, Jeeves. Gates-arita?"

Alfred's smile was brief, and cold. "I'll pass, thank you. May I?" Without seeming to move, he took the model from the parole officer's hands, hefted it, and thumbed a jeweler's loupe from his pocket. Silently he examined the horse from head to tail, back to stomach. Several times before he appeared satisfied. "Ah, such craftsmanship. Leonardo da Vinci's last commission for the Duke of Milan. Irreplaceable."

Gates didn't care. "Hey, Mr. French, I'm delirious for you. Now where's my cut?"

Crude, Hawk thought; there was something about the Englishman he didn't like at all. The winter in his voice wasn't limited to how he spoke; it was clearly part of something inside. Hawk knew this wasn't someone Gates should bait.

He was right.

Without a hint of expression, Alfred smashed the model over the cop's head and, while Gates staggered back toward the punch-bowl table, sifted through the debris until he found what he was looking for. Hawk didn't see it clearly, but it appeared to be a piece of crystal more intricately designed than he thought was possible.

Angrily Gates brushed at his hair with one hand while the other clenched into a threatening fist. "Why you sonofa—I don't believe this! You cheerio your way into my house—"

Alfred raised an eyebrow, but only dropped the crystal shard into his pocket.

"I ought to take Big Ben and shove it up your limey blimey bunghole!"

Uh-oh, Hawk thought, big mistake, jerk.

He was right again.

A very long, slender blade slid smoothly out of Alfred's sleeve into his hand.

Gates stomped toward him, his fist and voice raised. "Like I said, where's my c—"

And Alfred turned smoothly in a tight circle, his hand flashing out and back so rapidly, it was impossible to follow. A thin red line was left in its wake, along the cop's neck under his jaw.

No one moved.

Hawk's left hand drifted involuntarily to his own throat.

Then blood spurted from the wound, and Gates clutched frantically at the gash, gagging, turning, finally collapsing onto the table, which crumpled beneath his weight, bringing down the punch bowl, glasses, and stereo atop his body. A moment later the poker-playing dogs dropped from the wall to serve as his shroud.

"So much for his cut," Alfred said blandly. Chuckled. "Excuse my dry British humor."

Hawk had had enough, but the chair was too deep for him to climb out of in a hurry.

Cesar had no such trouble. He rose and nodded his approval. "Lovely work, Alfred. Are you taking the Concorde back?"

The Englishman wiped the blade clean with a soft cloth from his pocket. "Indeed I am, Mr. Mario. I'm really racking up those frequent flyer points."

"Hey look," Hawk said, desperately trying to clamp down on the hysteria he felt climbing around his heart, "I hate to interrupt you two lovebirds but—"

"Y'know," Antony remarked offhandedly as he and his brother stepped around the body and headed for the door, "I think Gates here promised Hawk a cut too."

The door closed quietly.

A year-long second passed in silence.

Then alarms in his head made Hawk try a second time to scramble to his feet, but lost his balance in the process and fell back into the chair, eyes growing wide when Alfred turned and raised his arm.

Not, Hawk thought, the way I'd have chosen.

The blade vanished into the spring-sheath tucked under the sleeve.

Hawk refused to take a breath.

Then Alfred held out his hand and Hawk eyed it warily before allowing himself to be pulled to his feet. The man was strong too; he'd scarcely flexed a muscle.

"Ta-ta, Hudson Hawk," the Englishman said.

"Too-doo-loo," Hawk replied breathlessly, waited several minutes after the man had left before getting out of there himself. The way his luck was running, there was probably a cop waiting on the doorstep, a warrant in one hand and a loaded gun in the other.

There wasn't.

And no one in the streets.

Which was fine with him. There had been a couple of unanswered questions before this affair had even begun tonight; now there were a dozen more.

Not the least of which was: who the hell was Alfred?

By the time he reached the 5-Tone, however, he had no more answers than he'd had when he started.

Which ticked him off.

And Tommy, just by sitting calmly on a bar stool and reading a newspaper, ticked him off too.

His friend grinned. "Did I miss anything?"

Hawk grabbed a couple of seconds to calm himself in case he lost it and grabbed the man's throat. "Gates blackmails me right outside the damn prison, you drive up: 'Did I miss anything?' Gates gets killed in his own apartment: 'Did I miss anything?' You probably went up to Mrs. Lincoln at Ford's Theater and said, 'How was the show? Did I miss anything?' "

Messina folded the paper and put it to one side. "Hey, no age jokes. Gates was killed, huh? Who do we send the thank-you note to?"

Hawk didn't laugh. He vaulted the bar and began fiddling with the cappuccino machine, trying to get it to give him some elixir.

"The butler did it," he answered, frustration growing when the machine wouldn't do what it was told. He whacked it and tried again. "Guy was a cross between Alistair Cooke and a Cuisinart. Dude took Mr. Ed and humpty-dumptied it over Gates." Another snarl of exasperation. "He said it was made by—get this, man—Leonardo—"

"Da Vinci. Ah yes." Messina sniffed aristocratically, and assumed a bored lecturer's voice. "A rare Renaissance piece. Da Vinci's 'Sforza,' I believe. An equestrian model of a never-executed statue. Actually, I consider it to be the prize of tonight's auction of objets d'equestrian." He paused. "Horse things."

Hawk jumped back when the machine produced sparks instead of cappuccino, then turned to his friend. "Okay, Mr. PBS, you got me."

Messina waved the newspaper at him. "Morning edition. Seems two daring thieves attempted to steal it last night, but thanks to three courageous guards, it will indeed be ready for the auction tonight."

Hawk closed his eyes briefly. "Attempted. Attempted? I did not want to steal that horse in the first place, remember, but I do have my pride. Face it, Tommy, when it comes to burglary and sex, I ..." He grabbed the paper from Messina's hand and spread it out on the bar. The central picture was of the three security guards, posing behind a table on which sat the "Sforza." It didn't help that a closer look revealed the thumbcuffs still on Mac and Jerry.

"This I do not understand."

Tommy swept the paper away. "Forget it, man. I mean, why try?" A pause. A breath. "Eddie, you know the game. What are you knocking yourself out for?"

Hawk vaulted the bar again and stared at the door, and the early morning beyond. "Because, Tommy, I am tired of not understanding things." He turned around, not caring that Tommy took a step back. "Cops, Mafia, and butlers forcing me to commit a crime that now it appears I didn't commit at all."

The line had been crossed again.

Tommy said nothing.

Hawk looked at the bar, at the recalcitrant machine, at the floor. Then he looked up without raising his head. "Let me ask you a question. How much does a new tuxedo cost?"

"What?" Messina tried to smile. "You're not thinking of actually going to this. Leave it alone, Hawk, leave it alone. We got a saloon to run. Together. Look, I'll put Captain Bob's steering wheel back up—"

"How much," Hawk repeated flatly, "does a new tuxedo cost?"

Tommy stared at him.

Hawk stared back.

"Okay," Tommy said at last. "You go if you want to go to the auction. But I'll be a son of a bitch if I'm paying for a new tuxedo."

No problem, Hawk thought, and heard no more of the man's protests.

After a couple of hours quick sleep, he was going back to the Rutherford.

And once he was there, somebody, somehow, was going to let him know what the hell was going on.

8

Garage sales, Hawk thought, have nothing on this.

He paused momentarily at the entrance to the Rutherford House's primary sales auditorium, self-consciously dusting at his blazer. The chairs were arranged theater style before the stage, and their occupants, in dress and manner, quite clearly had more money than he had ever seen, and would probably ever have, in his life. Each held a thick catalogue in his lap, and a small paddle that was raised—sometimes quickly, sometimes almost half-heartedly—when a bid was made. Conversation was low and intense; the lights were concentrated on the current for-sale item placed on a table beside the auctioneer's lectern. Just below the stage was a longer table behind which sat a number of men and women manning telephones.

A glance up as someone brushed past him revealed a high, ornate ceiling, and here and there an ornamental horse or unicorn hanging from a light chain. In honor, he supposed, of tonight's main event.

All too aware of the excitement in the room, at a pitch so high the place seemed charged with static electricity, he rolled his shoulders to settle his blazer, put on a don't-mind-the-clothes-I-belong-here-no-kidding expression, and headed down the center aisle, searching for an empty seat. As he did, he watched the customers, not expecting to find a familiar face but preparing not to be surprised in case he did.

The auctioneer, bald and as seemingly possessed as Alfred the so-called butler, nodded imperiously each time a paddle was raised.

"Fan*tas*tic example of Florentine marble," he said as one of his assistants lifted the next item on the agenda. Hawk nearly choked when the man added, "Who will begin at one hundred and sixty thousand? One hundred and sixty thousand?" A paddle floated. "One hundred eighty thousand."

It didn't take him long to realize that an inadvertent scratch of one's nose, or a finger wave to a friend, could cost some unlucky patron close to a million dollars, with no refunds. The idea made him nervous. A seat was what he needed, now, before he ended up with a magnificent example of Florentine marble to bring back to the 5-Tone.

Down toward the stage he spotted an empty one and moved swiftly toward it. On the way, he passed a rock star whose name he didn't remember but whose garish gold-and-silver-stud outfits were evidently an important part of his success. He seemed to be enjoying himself; his entourage obviously would have been happier in a kennel. He saw a large man in a rich, too-small suit, possibly Egyptian, although the teenage girl sitting beside him, in her more than all-American outfit, done in all-American hooker, was revealing enough to make Hawk stumble. By the time he reached the seat and sank gratefully into it, he had also spotted a Nordic blonde in a tiara worth at least as much as the city's deficit.

Amazing, he thought.

"One hundred ninety thousand," the auctioneer said emotionlessly.

Hawk scanned the crowd again, then snapped his face front when an extraordinarily beautiful woman squeezed past him and took the next seat. He inhaled. His heart thumped once, loudly.

"Sold."

The assistants bustled the object out of sight.

The woman adjusted herself.

Hawk exchanged a smile. "All these years of attending auctions," he said, "and I still get goose bumps. The paintings, the sculptures . . . the things that aren't really paintings or sculptures."

She answered, but she didn't turn around: "The pretentious vultures who don't even look up from their calculators to see what they're buying. Now that gives me goose bumps. Auctions are disgusting."

A quick sidestep. "I couldn't agree more. Savages."

She smiled, laughed, then cut herself off.

"Lot fifteen," the auctioneer announced. "An equestrian sconce attributed to the Cellini school."

Hawk checked the crowd again, and again saw

no one he recognized. He didn't know if that was a good sign or not.

"Sold," the auctioneer intoned, "to the caller from Newfoundland."

The winglike sound of turning pages.

"And finally," the auctioneer announced, "lot number seventeen, thought lost in the war, and again last night. The da Vinci 'Sforza,' the jewel of the sale." As a begowned and bejeweled woman held the model up with white-gloved hands, he added, "Fan*tas*tic."

Hawk laughed silently and shook his head. He had to admit it—whatever was going on, whatever the scam was, whoever was behind it had more balls than the Mets.

He glanced at the Venus beside him. "Is looking like a constipated warthog a prerequisite to getting a job in the art world?"

The auctioneer cleared his throat noisily. "There have naturally been questions of its authenticity, so to verify, we have Dr. Anna Baragli, of the Vatican. Doctor?"

Hawk looked around for the eminent doctor as did all the others, then held back a whimper when the woman beside him stood. With a pained smile he moved his legs to allow her to pass, and decided to find the nearest hole to crawl into when she paused long enough to whisper, "Some of us warthogs are more constipated than others."

Class, he thought as she made her way to the stage, you've really got class, Hawkins. You jerk.

During the wait, he began to think that maybe it was time to leave. The moment she took a look at the "Sforza," she would know it was a fake, and he didn't think he wanted to tell her that the original, the real one, had been busted over the head of a guy who served Gates-aritas. She didn't appear to be the kind who would understand.

She held it up.

He held his breath.

She examined it from every angle with a large magnifying glass, and he didn't miss the quickly hidden expression that darted across her face.

He closed his eyes. The shit, he told himself, is about to hit the—

"Fantastic!" she exclaimed.

He opened his eyes.

"Perfection," she added proudly. "The Vatican extends its jealousy to the lucky bidder."

He blinked several times to be sure he hadn't fallen into a coma.

The auctioneer thanked her with a condescending nod, and turned away as if she no longer existed. "We will begin the bidding at two and a half million dollars."

A paddle.

"To you, sir, eighty-three. Ninety—your bid, madam—ninety point five."

More questions, Hawk thought, I hate questions. It's like being back in school, with the nuns at St. Agnes.

He slipped into the aisle as Dr. Baragli left the stage and stood by the telephone table. She picked up a receiver and whispered something into it.

A deep voice from the back cried, "One hundred million clammo, Franco!"

A glance in that direction almost threw him off-course. The man he had seen on the magazine cover the night before, Darwin Mayflower, was strolling down the aisle, attending to the crowd as if they had come solely to see him. He laughed, he kissed, he shook hands, he waved; he high-fived the rock star and planted a lascivious kiss on the young hooker.

"One hundred million dollars to Mr. Darwin Mayflower," said the auctioneer.

Just in case, Hawk supposed sourly, there was a dead man around who didn't hear it the first time.

As Mayflower finally took his place in the reserved section near the front, his wife made her own entrance. Hawk wasn't sure about the clothes—they were outrageous enough to be expensive and ugly enough to be more expensive—but he recognized the monster Tiffany watch she wore, even if he never knew one of them came attached to a leash that, in turn, was attached to one of the most obnoxious-looking little dogs he'd seen outside the prison yard.

"Francesco, one hundred million and one."

Mayflower clasped a hand to his wounded heart. The audience laughed.

"Outbid by my own wench," he moaned loudly. *"Quelle bummere."*

Minerva Mayflower blew him a wet kiss. "Don't hate me, baby." Then, to the dog, "Here, Bunny."

Bunny, Hawk thought, perfect.

"Fan*tastic*," the auctioneer declared. "The bid is at one hundred million and one dollars."

The moment the amount sunk in, a tiny alarm began to chime in Hawk's head. This was too right, too much of a coincidence. As he turned to make sure Anna Baragli hadn't left, he saw the Mayflowers billing and cooing at each other.

"Ladies and gentlemen?" the auctioneer said.

His assistant held the model up again.

No one else offered a paddle.

Later, Hawk promised the couple; this was something he wasn't going to pass up, even though, for now, he didn't exactly know why.

A door opened in the side wall.

"Going," the auctioneer warned.

Hawk stopped again, this time because of the guard standing in the doorway.

It was Big Stan.

Who immediately recognized him and pulled out his gun.

"Going," the auctioneer promised.

Hawk instantly swiveled around again, knowing that running away would attract too much attention.

Stan, however, didn't see it that way.

Hawk watched him from the corner of his eye, and stopped yet again when Anna Baragli's foot suddenly found its way in front of the guard's ankle.

Stan fell.

Hawk, beginning to feel like a windup toy gone berserk, turned back to the stage just as the auctioneer said, "Gone!"

The gavel came down.

The Mayflowers ducked out of their chairs.

Hawk just had time to throw up a protective arm when the lectern exploded.

The next few moments were confusion, and terror.

Hawk found himself on the floor, staring up at the ceiling where some dangling ornaments were swaying dangerously on their chains, and others had already plummeted into the screaming crowd. He shook his head to clear it of the blast's effect and pushed painfully to his feet. A check uncovered no injuries, but he couldn't say the same for the rest of them—faces were bleeding, women and men were moaning, and as he struggled back toward the place where he last saw Anna, the Mayflowers breezed past arm in arm, not a hair or fold out of place.

The dog barked at him from Mrs. Mayflower's arm.

With cries for ambulances and the police replacing many of the panicked screams, he assisted one old man to his feet, helped a tattered but uninjured woman into a chair he righted with one hand. Then he saw Anna sway into sight and he pushed his way through the crowd toward her. She didn't appear to be hurt aside from a few smudges and scratches, and he was about to wave for her attention when movement made him look up.

One of the unicorns had begun to work loose of its mooring.

He called out; she didn't hear him.

He shoved his way out of the aisle and used the chairs to leapfrog toward the stage.

The unicorn fell.

Without thinking, he launched himself toward her, catching her with his shoulder and knocking her clear as the plaster beast crashed on the spot where she'd been standing. She cried out as she fell, but when he rolled over and sat up, he could see she was all right.

He smiled.

Her answer was an outstretched hand that he took, and together they managed to regain their feet and dust themselves off as best they could.

He didn't see Stan.

A check of the demolished stage told him there was probably nothing left of the auctioneer but his bald.

Anna took his arm.

He was grateful. It gave him the opportunity to play the gentleman and, at the same time, not fall flat on his face. His head hurt, his hip hurt where it had collided with the floor, his back hurt, and when he thought about it, it would probably be easier to figure out what didn't hurt than did.

They moved up the aisle, stepping gingerly over debris and making sure that the ceiling held no more surprises.

"My God," she said, "that was bold of you. You didn't have to do that."

He eased a babbling young man out of their way. "It was nothing. Anybody would have done the same thing. It's an impulse."

Her lips twisted sourly. "No, I meant you didn't have to tackle me and rip my dress. A polite push, perhaps? A clear shout of 'Watch out, Anna' would have done nicely."

He almost left her. "Well, excuse me, Milady. I would have flown over and carried you up to a pink cloud but I left my cape at the cleaners."

His pique subsided the minute her finger touched

his lips, and the sour smile was replaced by a genuine one.

She'd been kidding.

"Thanks, tough guy. Thanks a lot."

He shrugged.

"Why was that guard chasing you?"

It took no time at all to decide that a straight answer wasn't going to endear him to her.

"Because danger, Doc, is my middle—"

She gasped and looked up.

He looked up and had no time to duck when a Pegasus as large as her unicorn slammed onto his head.

9

Hawk decided he wanted to go back to prison. Not only was it more comfortable there, but his fellow inmates weren't nearly as dangerous as the people he'd been meeting on the outside. He also didn't hurt as much. In addition to the list he'd been making while at the auction house, he could now add several more areas of his body that, given half a chance, would defect to someone else.

It would, all in all, be a lot better if he were dead.

Unless, of course, he already was dead.

He certainly felt like it.

He could even see what could only be an angel, hovering somewhere just beyond the reach of his considerably blurred vision.

That was okay.

Dead meant not having to be shot at anymore, or having things thrown at him, or people chasing him, or jumping off buildings at a single bound so people chasing him wouldn't be able to shoot at him anymore.

He might even get to see Little Eddie again.

He groaned when his body bounced unexpectedly.

Air turbulence in heaven; something he'd never thought of before.

The angel shifted.

He blinked, his vision cleared, and he decided that God must be in serious trouble if He had to resort to angels who looked like Cesar Mario.

Unless he was in . . .

"Am . . . I in hell?"

"Not quite," Cesar said with an evil grin. "But close."

"Thirty seconds and counting," his brother told him.

"If," said Cesar, "you know what we mean."

Although Antony nodded, Hawk just knew deep down that the jerk didn't mean it. "Couldn't just play along, could you, Eddie."

Another bounce, and an abrupt shift of the world, and Hawk's mind cleared. He glanced around and realized that he was in an ambulance, that it was still night, and that he was strapped to a gurney. He refused to let himself ask questions. Instead, he began to test the straps holding his wrists, noting as he did the usual array of equipment in the back, and a tray of syringes on a low shelf beside him.

Cesar grinned. "Pretty classy way of covering our tracks, huh."

Antony preened. "I think that auctioneer landed at LaGuardia."

"Subtlety," the elder Mario said, "was never one of our strong points."

"Neither's flossing," Hawk muttered.

Antony frowned his puzzlement and touched at

his teeth with his gun hand. Hawk yanked his right hand free at the same time, grabbed the tray, and flung it at the thug's face. The tray bounced off his forehead; the syringes didn't—several of them remained stuck, quivering, in his flesh.

He screamed as he fell, the gun firing wildly.

The ambulance lurched.

Hawk scrambled for the other strap while Cesar, incensed and trying to avoid his brother writhing on the floor, grabbed the gurney, obviously intending to climb over Hawk and take his head off.

The ambulance swerved violently, throwing the mobster off-balance. To stop himself, he grabbed the gurney's back and pulled.

The gurney moved.

Hawk moved.

The rear doors opened and the gurney flew out.

Hawk braced himself for the worst, but the sheet caught the door and he, and the gurney, suddenly became part of the ambulance's wild flight across the Brooklyn Bridge. He grabbed onto the edges, eyes watering in the wind that slammed viciously into his face. He could feel, but could barely see, the vehicle swinging from side to side, bouncing off cars unable to get away in time, straightening, then veering sharply again.

He looked at the sheet and wondered if he could pull himself close enough to get back inside. He couldn't tell what the brothers were doing because the door kept slapping open and shut, but it had to be better than this. He knew that at any moment he was going to sideswipe a car, or the railing, and nothing would be able to save him.

The sheet ripped.

He stared at it.

The sheet tore.

He swallowed heavily and held on more tightly.

The sheet flapped away over his head, and the gurney snapped to one side, momentum carrying him into a lane of his own. Body English didn't do a thing, and aside from the cars that narrowly got out of his path, he saw that he was heading for a toll plaza, all of whose lanes were blocked by large, steel, striped barrier arms.

Life, he thought, don't get much better than this.

Jump or ride; either way he was dead.

The ambulance fell behind, still swinging uncontrollably through the traffic.

A convertible pulled up alongside him, and he figured, why not? it can't get any weirder than this.

He looked; it was filled with girls.

"Hey," one of them called, "is this a fraternity thing?"

Hawk blinked dumbly.

"You're cute," another one said. "Are you going to die?"

"No," he said, "but I'm willing to try anything once."

Jesus Christ, can they *see*?

"Are you premed?"

He stammered, maybe he nodded, but he definitely tried to convey to them that he, and very possibly they, were going to Forest Lawn in the next thirty seconds if something wasn't done.

"Too bad," the girl answered sadly. "I only date laywers."

The convertible peeled off, tires screeching, the girls waving to him gaily.

For this, he thought, I left Sing Sing.

Then he groaned when he realized he was heading directly for the exact change lane; the gate was down.

Frantically, not knowing if he was being overly optimistic or just plain stupid, he braced himself on his right arm and released his left hand, fumbled into his pocket and yanked out a palmful of coins.

He didn't bother to aim.

He flung the change ahead of him and lowered his face to the gurney bed, praying fervently, feeling time slow down around him, daring a look up just as the coins rattled into the plastic basket, just as the red light turned green, and the arm shuddered upward.

He felt its breath as it missed his head by less than an inch.

Cesar panicked when Hawk and the gurney were snatched out of his hand. He stumbled forward to the open partition between the back and the driver's cab. The driver, obviously hysterical, tried desperately to keep the vehicle in line, but the ambulance had a mind of its own.

Cesar screamed at him.

The driver screamed back.

A small car ran up on the pedestrian walkway; another made a complete three-sixty in order to get out of the way.

Antony groaned behind them.

Cesar looked frantically, eyes widening in disbelief when the gurney swept by them, several lanes to his right.

He shouted.

The driver shouted.

The toll plaza was chaos, but the driver somehow managed to thread his way safely through the traffic, aiming for the nearest gap and the highway beyond.

Cesar didn't flinch when they smashed through the gate, then pointed when the gurney and that goddamn Hawk nearly cut them off.

"Turn him into roadkill!" he ordered.

Antony poked his syringe-pocked face through the partition: "Yeah, run him down!"

The driver looked at him and screamed.

Cesar looked at him and screamed.

Then they looked through the windshield.

And all of them screamed as the ambulance tried and failed to avoid a car stalled in the middle of the road. The ambulance struck it near the back, jackknifed, and exploded before it ever touched the ground again.

Hawk cringed at the explosion, dared only a quick look over his shoulder before the gurney swerved onto an off-road.

Jump or ride, he thought again, jump or ride.

The road angled slightly up and left.

The gurney began to slow down.

Within seconds, before he really knew what had happened, he had come to a halt in the darkness beneath an overpass. A darkness not quite complete, touched as it was by the still-burning wreckage of the ambulance and the Mario brothers.

He lay there with his mouth open, gulping for air, trying to get some feeling back into his limbs. When he felt as if he could move without anything falling off, he rolled off to his feet. His legs protested. He sat immediately and felt the night air begin to freeze the sweat dripping from his face.

Jesus, he thought, Jesus.

He lowered his head and forced calm to replace the certainty of his dying. It wasn't easy. First he had to convince himself that he was still alive and didn't really need to throw up; then he had to assure himself that he just wasn't dreaming that he was still alive; lastly, he had to believe that what had just happened was a miracle, don't question it, just be grateful.

A muffled explosion momentarily lightened the shadows.

He shuddered.

In the distance, the urgent cry of a siren.

He wiped his face with his sleeves, rubbed at his eyes, and was about to push himself to his feet when he saw movement in the darkness opposite him, just to the left of a canted, discarded Porta Potti propped against the stone wall.

No more, he thought wearily, God, please, no more.

A slender young man stepped into the flickering light, dressed in black, his eyes hidden behind wire-rim glasses. He carried a stainless-steel suitcase that he lowered to the ground and opened.

Not a word.

Hawk was too dazed to speak.

The man pulled out a cellular telephone and began to speak, too low for Hawk to catch any of the words.

Not, Hawk decided, from the auto club.

The man looked up.

A faint whirring sound, and Hawk saw a second man, similarly dressed, gliding down a wire affixed to the bridge's underside. He said nothing. He walked over to Hawk and held out a card. As Hawk took it, he saw the man's hands—across the fingers of one was tattooed HATE; across the other, FROG.

A car horn blared above him.

Blinking rapidly, he stared at the card until the words on it made sense: *My name is Kit Kat. This is not a dream.*

I wouldn't bet on it, he muttered silently, but when he tried to stand, Kit Kat chopped him lightly on the side of the neck to put him back down.

He was too tired to fight, and too hurt to feel hurt.

The young man replaced the phone in the suitcase and pulled out what looked disturbingly like a fancy cattle prod.

"This," Hawk said to him, "is the worst night—"

"When it rains it pours," the man said amiably. "Name's Snickers. The plane leaves in forty."

The prod touched Hawk's leg.

Instantly every muscle contracted, and though he felt the pain, it was too intense for him to scream; he curled into a ball to escape further assault. The best he could do was groan, and groan again when a third person joined the party. Though his sight was still blurred, he could see she was pretty, black, and young.

She smiled coyly at him and winked prettily. "Name's Almond Joy. I know, pretty silly," she added as he uncurled stiffly and tried to push himself back into a sitting position, "but it's better than when we first started out. Our code names were diseases. You don't know what it's like to be called Clymidia for a year."

Somehow he couldn't feel it in his heart to sympathize. He was halfway to standing when she said, "Oh. I forgot." Walked over and kicked him onto his back.

There was no temper left in him.

H wanted to be angry, he wanted to strike back, but his confusion, as much as his injuries, had finally sapped his strength and most of his will. The best he could do was roll painfully to his hands and knees, and think nothing of it when the Porta Potti door opened and a man stepped out. At least Hawk thought it was a man. It had two arms and two legs, but it was so goddamn big, he couldn't be sure. And he could only stare in amazement when the door slammed shut, catching the tail of the man's coat. The man kept moving, unaware of what had happened until he had dragged it behind him for a good ten feet. He stopped, confused. Moved again, and suddenly whirled to see what was back there.

The Porta Potti fell on top of him.

Hawk considered laughing, but it would have hurt too much.

The big man extricated himself without help from his friends and walked over to Hawk, who decided that this one was going to sit on him to death.

"Name's Butterfingers," the giant rumbled.

"No shit," Hawk answered.

Without any perceptible effort, Butterfingers picked him up and propped him against the gurney.

At that moment a man in a wide-lapeled suit and panama hat joined the other four.

Wear a sign that says spy, why not, Hawk thought as he tried to put himself back in order.

The new one smiled at him sadly. "Man, don't you just hate kids."

"George," Almond Joy protested, "you promised. No old CIA/new CIA jokes."

The man ignored her. "I call them the MTV IA," he said. "Punks still think the Bay of Pigs is an herbal tea. They think the Cold War involves penguins and—"

Hawk held up a hand—*hang on a minute, hang on.* His eyes narrowed. "Don't I know you?" There was something about him, something about his face and the way he talked out of the side of his thin-lipped mouth.

The man shrugged. "You might." He beamed without warmth and showed his profile. "I'm the guy who tricked you into robbing a government installation and had you sent to prison for it."

Hawk straightened.

"Of course, at the time," the man continued blithely, "I was bald with a beard, no mustache, and I had a slightly different nose."

Damn, Hawk thought, Cesar was right.

"So if you don't recognize me, I won't be offended."

Damn right, Hawk thought, amazed at the rage stirring somewhere inside, you'll be dead.

Then he knew, and the shock of recognition almost choked him. "George. George Kaplan! You bastard, you're gonna need another nose—"

He exploded from the gurney, and froze when each of the Candy Bars pulled a gun.

"But," he continued easily, "I'm not the type of guy to hold a grudge."

Kaplan wasn't amused. He jammed his hands into his pockets and ordered the others with a jerk of his head to put their weapons away. "I used you as a diversion. While you were getting captured upstairs, I was shredding documents in the basement. Deep down, I guess, I was just jealous. You were one incredible thief."

Right, Hawk thought, tell me another one.

"To what do I owe the dishonor of a reunion, you centrally intelligent scumsicle?"

Kaplan tossed a friendly arm around his shoulder. "I want to make things up to you."

Hawk felt as if he were being embraced by a cobra—his skin crawled uncontrollably, and every warning bell throughout his system clanged unmercifully, and loudly. But he didn't take his gaze from the man's face, not even when his peripheral vision caught Snickers and Butterfingers wrestling a huge suitcase out of the shadows.

"That," said Kaplan, "is why I got you this gig, doll. And to quote Karen Carpenter, 'We've only just begun.' "

"Three minutes twenty-three," Hawk said automatically. "Kaplan, if you think I'm going to do another—"

"Hush," said Kaplan. "My employer wants a meeting."

"Employer? The President?"

The man chuckled. "No. Someone powerful. Oh," he said, staring at the bottom of the overpass. "Look. What's that up there?"

Hawk rolled his eyes. "I'm supposed to fall for that?"

Kaplan sighed. "Shucks, guess not."

Before Hawk could move then, the man belted him with a blackjack. He stumbled backward, all control gone and consciousness fading. But not before he felt himself being stuffed into the suitcase.

Then he was gone.

Nothing felt at all.

10

There was no time for reflection, speculation, or fear.

One moment the lights had gone off; the next he found himself lying on a supremely uncomfortable couch that seemed more wood than upholstery.

And someone had put him in a new suit of clothes. New, and very expensive.

He stared down at himself, his right hand touching the lapels, the shirt, not understanding a thing except that he hadn't died. Again. It was getting monotonous.

A check of the room without moving his head revealed nothing. There were no decorations, no carpeting, nothing but him and the couch and a place with ridiculously high ceilings and too much ornate plaster.

His eyes closed.

Opened.

The room, and the clothes, hadn't gone away.

All right, he thought, and took his time getting

to his feet, making sure everything worked. He had no watch, but knew that a fair amount of time had passed. His aches had either gone or had subsided to periodic dull throbs; a brush of a palm across his jaw told him he needed a shave, but not badly; and his stomach told him he hadn't eaten in too damn long.

A nod.

Another look to be sure the freaks in black weren't around, and he moved slowly toward the door. Kaplan didn't work for the CIA? In a pig's knuckle. Working for someone else on the side? The man didn't have the imagination. The Mario brothers? He shook his head as he pulled the door open. No; and if he did, he was fresh out of luck and a job.

So who—

He stepped outside and gaped.

Stepped down a few stone steps on a long staircase and turned in a slow, disbelieving circle.

No, he thought.

At the bottom of the staircase, moving toward him, was Alfred the deadly butler.

No, he thought.

He looked up at the buildings, down at the paving-stone sidewalk, at the incredibly ancient buildings across the way.

Italy? he wondered.

"No. Way."

"Welcome to Rome, sir," Alfred said.

"Yes way."

And let himself be guided down the stairs to the door of a limousine large enough to house the population of a small but wealthy country. When Alfred opened the door, Hawk didn't argue; he only took one more look to be sure it really wasn't Brooklyn, and slid in. And would have slid right back out again, except that as soon as he sat down the limousine pulled smoothly, soundlessly into the street.

Hawk looked to the roof. You really hate me, don't you?

Darwin Mayflower shook his unresisting hand while, at the same time, he blustered into a telephone receiver.

"For those kind of wages, I could have built the factory in America! They're Vietnamese! Do they know they're Vietnamese? I mean, can't we just give them Bart Simpson T-shirts? I hear depressing news like this, I want to commit suicide." He slammed the receiver down. "Alfred, hold my calls." A large welcoming smile flashed at Hawk. "So, Hawk! The Hawkster! What do you think of the vehicle?"

Hawk hated to admit it, but he was impressed. "You could hold American Bandstand in here. Why did you duck at the auction, asshole?"

"Because I didn't want to get hurt, taterhead." Mayflower shrugged elaborately, still holding the smile when a fax machine pinged to announce an incoming message. "What can I tell you, I'm the villain. Initially it was a priority to keep a lot of buffers between you and me, but since most of them are dead now, I figured what the heck." He laughed. Sobered. "Hawk, you come highly recommended. I would have done things differently at the auction house but, hey, I want to be in business with you."

Mayflower grabbed the fax from the machine,

scanned it, scowled, and shoved it into a shredder built into the door.

I am mad, Hawk thought then; I thought I was mad before, but now I'm really mad.

"Look," he said as the telephone rang, "my life is not some deal. I—"

"It's Boston, Mr. Mayflower," Alfred said from the front seat.

Mayflower lifted a hand apologetically. "Sorry, but I have to take this. Those are valid points, though."

Hawk couldn't believe it. Mayflower was either the stupidest jackass in the world, or the most arrogant. But he wasn't prepared for the viciousness in the man's voice.

"You better have a good excuse . . . you better have a better excuse! You are so weak! I'm only thankful your ancestors didn't settle America, or I'd have to change my name to Running Brave or Vomiting Antelope. Really. Well, now listen close, Daddio—" And he held the earpiece over the armrest, pressed a button, and a piercing shriek filled the car.

Hawk gasped.

The driver coasted the car to the curb and stopped.

Mayflower nodded. "Shall we?"

He left without looking back and Hawk considered waiting for Alfred to take him back to the real world. Then, curiosity and his temper working against him, he followed Mayflower up the steps of an immense marble and granite structure that reminded him of the days when Hitler and El Duce thought they knew what good taste was.

A temptation to bolt and run was stifled when he noted that the Englishman, aloof and deadly, brought up the rear.

"So, Hawkasaurus, I won't mince words," Mayflower said.

"Whatever," Hawk grumbled. "You own Boardwalk, you own Park Place, you own the four railroads. You think you're God. For all I know, you're probably right." Closer to the entrance the building was even uglier and more depressing. "I just wanted to have a cappuccino," he continued forlornly, almost talking to himself, "maybe play some Nintendo after I found out what the hell it was." Frustrated, he grabbed for Mayflower's arm. "Why the hell didn't you just *buy* the damn horse? What am I saying, you *did* buy it."

Mayflower flicked the hand away as if it were no more than a summer fly. "Oh, let me see . . . there are organizations that think we wanted the 'Sforza' for reasons other than putting it in the Da Vinci museum we're building in Vinci. Hopefully, those organizations think our plan has been ruined with the explosion of our replica."

Hawk only stared at him, hoping that sooner or later the jerk would start to speak recognizable English.

"If I seem vague, Hawk, grand. We want a low profile on this, that's why I got Kaplan and the Candy Bars involved. I helped George help the Mario brothers and Gates get you out."

Hawk wasn't sure he heard the man correctly. "What? You got me out of jail? You?" He considered that for a moment, and almost made himself dizzy. "So, boss, you going to tell me what that crystal piece inside the horse means?"

He kept his expression neutral when Mayflower glared at him, and said, "Way to go, Alfie! How many people did you break that thing in front of? Good help's hard to find."

Hawk lifted an eyebrow. "I guess that's a no, huh."

Mayflower didn't respond. He only led him down a long marble hallway and into a massive room. Hawk checked his stride while Mayflower charged ahead, gesturing happily at a group of people seated at a mammoth M-shaped conference table above which hung a portrait of the Mayflowers—including the disgusting little dog—in a style usually reserved for world conquerors and long-lived royalty.

Then he saw Minerva.

"Ladies and gentlemen of the board," Mayflower announced grandly.

His wife, in heels and a black outfit designed to stop the heart of any normal, and a dozen subnormal, males, lay sprawled atop the table wearing a headset from which Hawk thought he heard music, unless it was a tape of tortured chickens.

"And, Minerva," Mayflower added with a loving, scolding look, "let's give it up for Hudson Hawk."

They applauded politely, nearly a score of them ranging, he noted, from an Indian prince who couldn't have been more than nine or ten, to a sweet elderly woman who was so sweet and so gentle-seeming he figured she probably carried a chain saw in her beaded purse.

"Hello," Minerva called cheerfully. "Bunny, ball-ball."

She tossed a small ball into the air that Bunny scurried to catch as it skidded across the highly polished floor.

Hawk did his best not to kick it into Greece, and moved cautiously toward the table, unable to take it in but trying nevertheless. His brain refused to work, however. Too much, too soon, too fast. He supposed this was what shell-shocked meant.

To add insult to injury, and not a little pain, one of the board members lifted a delicate cup of cappuccino to his lips and sipped, sighed, and sipped again.

Hawk decided that if he ever changed his profession to assassin, that one would be the first to die. For free.

"Hawkmeister," Mayflower called from the head of the table, "we got you clothes, a great hotel, and a 250,000 lira per diem."

Minerva sat up abruptly, scowling. "What? That's two hundred dollars a day! So he can get a hooker and some tequila? Veto, Darwin."

Hawk grinned at Mayflower. "Guess I know who wears the penis in this family."

Minerva glared. "For God's sake, chain this ... this convict."

Alfred yawned and pulled a pair of gleaming handcuffs from his pocket.

Hawk backed away a step. "Alfred, you're a very polite psychopath, but if you think—"

"Please, Mr. Hawkins, let's not be pathetic."

Pathetic.

Dumb, sometimes; stupid, plenty of times; thickheaded and stubborn; why not.

Pathetic?

Temper lashed his foot out toward the butler's kneecap, the force behind it enough to smash the bone to powder.

Or would have done if Alfred hadn't moved agilely to one side without seeming to move at all, and before Hawk could recoup and strike again, the Englishman slammed him across the table and into an empty chair. With the air gone from his lungs, he was helpless when Alfred pulled his hands behind his back and latched the cuffs in place.

The board applauded.

Lord, Hawk thought miserably, and nearly wept when Bunny decided there was something fascinating about his crotch.

Minerva leaned closer, ignoring the dog's sniffing explorations. "We want," she said, "da Vinci's sketchbook. What do they call it? The Codex."

Mayflower nodded his eager agreement. "Listen, Hawk, this might be difficult to believe, but I'm just a regular Joe who wants to be happy."

He waited.

Hawk eyed the dog suspiciously; it was, he decided, much too interested.

"However," Mayflower continued, "happiness comes from the achieving of goals. And when you make your first billion by the age of nineteen, it's hard to keep coming up with new goals. But now"— he sighed happily—"I have my new goal. It's called world domination, and with your help—Bunny, quit that!"

"Bunny!" Minerva snapped. "Ball-ball!"

Hawk shook his head. "Think he's already got his ball-balls, lady. Five more minutes, please, it's been so long."

Minerva gave him a long look of disgust and yanked the dog away.

Hawk glanced around the table. "Anybody got a cigarette?" When no one laughed, or even managed a smile, he sighed. "But seriously, do me a favor and Concorde me back to prison. I don't care anymore. I hope you have the receipts for these threads."

Minerva gave him a look that turned his stomach. "You go back, little man, I guarantee you won't be alone. You'll have a guinea barkeep cellmate. You're still young enough to have fun shanking child molesters for a pack of smokes, but Tommy 5-Tone will go in knowing that the next time he gets out it'll be to attend his own funeral." She shuddered happily. "Depressing."

Hawk didn't believe her. "You wouldn't risk the dime to call the police. You have no proof."

Smugly he watched Minerva turn her back, but didn't like it at all when Mayflower said, "Ah, the magic word."

As if responding to a cue, Alfred deposited a slide projector onto the table.

Well, Hawk thought.

Mayflower then clicked a series of slides onto the bare wall.

Hell, Hawk thought.

They were good, perfectly focused and in glorious color—of him and Tommy robbing Rutherford Auction House. Every step of the way. The board reacted with murmurs of approval and nods of appreciation for the professional work they witnessed.

"It's véjà du, Hawkhead," Mayflower said.

"Something you wish never happened. We shot the entire operation with hidden cameras behind the hidden cameras. Hired the guy who did the last *Sports Illustrated* swimsuit issue. Excellent work—oops, damn Fotomat assholes."

The last slide vanished so quickly, Hawk wasn't sure but that he saw Mayflower in flesh-tight panties and nippleless bra, while Minerva stood beside him in black leather. Alfred at the corner with a huge spiked paddle.

World domination, he thought, right.

The slide projector disappeared, and was replaced by what looked like elaborate annual report presentation folders given to each of the people around the table. Wriggling around in the chair allowed him to see the title: The da Vinci Alchemy Project.

Right, he thought again.

Then Minerva leaned over him and let him see her teeth.

It wasn't really a smile.

"My man," she said, wrinkling her nose at him, "you are going to hit a church."

11

Hawk couldn't decide whether to be nervous or awed, and finally, after the Mayflower limousine had circled St. Peter's Square for the second time, he managed a bit of both. The crowds, the vendors of food and papal souvenirs, the gawkers and those who prayed, and the sheer noise of it all even within the confines of the car were close to overwhelming. And once again, although he couldn't believe he had been trapped into pulling another job—and at this place yet!—the adrenaline began its work.

But not for all the reasons Mayflower and his people—including the two dark-faced flunkies seated opposite him—thought.

There was nothing he could do about the blackmail. The threat against Tommy was as strong as any bar he had seen in Sing Sing. But he could, somehow, try to foul things up in such a way that he couldn't take the blame. That way, everybody was off the hook, and Mayflower—not to mention

Kaplan and his weird Candy Bar team—would have no real reason to put him back in a cell. Or a grave.

And if you believe that, he thought with an abrupt attack of gloom, you'll probably clap your hands and wait for Tinker Bell to bring the cavalry.

A plan.

He needed a plan.

The limousine circled the square a third time.

"The Vatican," he said in amazement. "I can't believe I'm robbing the Vatican. The nuns at St. Agnes predicted I'd end up doing this."

The flunkies were not interested.

Hawk smiled at them as he pushed up his sunglasses with his middle finger.

Shortly afterward he trailed through what the tourist brochure called the Map Room. Others wandered about, whispering to each other in a dozen different languages; there were sleepy-eyed guards at each entrance. The centerpiece of the exhibit was a mural, vast and colorful, vibrantly portraying the world as it had been hundreds of years ago. He examined it thoughtfully; at the same time, he checked the room's dimensions, scowled to himself at the apparent lack of appropriate exits for people on the run from the police, and moved on, always making sure those ever-present flunkies weren't too close to cramp his style.

A notepad from his jacket pocket was scribbled in.

In another room, not as large as the first but just as crowded, a guard stood watch before a large painting of an unnamed pope performing a coronation. As Hawk feigned admiration of the artist's work, he said, "Hey, man."

The guard smiled. *"Buon giorno."*

Hawk checked over his shoulder. "Yeah, *buon giorno.* I'm being blackmailed into robbing the Vatican by a psychotic American corporation along with the CIA."

The guard looked at him, bewildered. "You're being ... uh, I don't ... I don't ..." His expression changed from bewildered to helpless.

"You don't speak English?" Hawk said, sighed, patted the guard's shoulder as he walked away. "You know, you have very beautiful eyes for a man."

More rooms, more halls, until he found himself in a corridor open on one side to the city around the Vatican. He scribbled another note as he checked the condition and distance of the rooftops across the way, then widened his eyes when he discovered a row of international telephone booths. He raced to the nearest one, checked to be sure his shadows weren't in sight, then grabbed up the receiver.

"Operator," he said urgently, "yes, I'm having a wonderful *buon giorno.* Look, I want to make a collect call to Tommy 5-Tone Messina, that's right, in New York."

The flunkies ghosted around the corner.

He slammed the receiver back onto its cradle, said, "My stockbroker," to the two men, and moved on.

Plan; where the hell is the damned plan?

Finally he turned in to a corridor filled with gilt-framed portraits, tapestries, ceiling murals, and a carpet so elegant he felt guilty walking along it. At the far end was an arched opening, and he slowed as he approached it, taking his time to note every inch of the floor, the walls, even the heavily ornate trim along the ceiling. By the time he reached the arch, he had scribbled enough to make a good start on his memoirs, checked his reflection in each of the gold-framed mirrors on either side of the opening, and realized there was nothing else he could do but carry on.

With a deep breath then, he stepped through to a landing at the top of a huge fan staircase.

Lord, he thought, oh . . . Lord.

This wasn't a room; this was heaven. Son of a gun, the nuns were right.

His gaze couldn't take it all in at once—the tall windows through which pure sunlight slanted and crossed, the worn marble staircase he descended and its twin leading up and out the other side, pedestals and alcoves topped and lined with saintly statuary, and a massive, eye-wateringly stunning chandelier hanging from the center of the vaulted, paneled ceiling, poised like a celestial arrow over a simple glass case made all the more inspiring by that simplicity.

Tourists in pairs, alone, and in escorted groups moved through the great room toward the case. Footsteps that should have cracked loudly on the mosaic marble floor were soft, as were the voices of the people who hovered around the display.

As if, he thought uncomfortably, they were in church.

He moved closer.

The display case was cordoned off by thick velvet ropes and flanked by two explanatory tablets, but he didn't have to read them to know that the ancient, leather-bound book contained inside was da

Vinci's Codex, open now to his familiar sketch of Man within the universal circle.

And this, he thought glumly, is what I'm supposed to steal?

Doomed; I'm doomed.

A woman's reverent voice carried in the room: "Here we enter the da Vinci Room. Are we all following? Leonardo is best-known as a painter. But it is his gift as an inventor who drew together science and art that is most incredible."

He turned, and couldn't help what he knew had to be a truly stupid grin from crossing his face.

Moving down the stairs with a group of obviously well-to-do tourists and their families, and carrying a portfolio bag in one hand, was Anna Baragli.

As the group huddled around the Codex, she smiled brightly when she saw him, reaching out and giving him a quick, surreptitious hand squeeze.

"Tough guy. What are you—how's your head?"

He felt like a teenager faced with a goddess. "Yes, and my giraffe loves it too."

She laughed and turned toward her charges. "As you know, the da Vinci Codex has lived in the Vatican for centuries and will continue to live here for centuries to come."

"That's what you think," he muttered before he could stop himself, and grinned inanely when she stared at him.

"Question, sir?"

He shrugged.

Her response was a quizzical lift of an eyebrow before she gestured toward the display. "His untiring pen predicted the airplane, the submarine, the bicycle, the helicopter, and even the tank."

Then from the middle of the group, a small child barged out and planted herself next to Hawk. She held a stuffed elephant in one hand. "This is so boring! Do you hate Italy as much as I do, Pokey?" Her voice changed for the toy's scratchy reply. "*Sí, señor.* Italy sucks the big one. Why can't we go to the Epcot Center?"

Hawk grimaced, and wondered if he'd get a reward for squashing the little brat.

Probably not, so he stepped away from the others and scanned the room again. A frown wrinkled on his brow. Something wasn't quite right, and he couldn't put his finger on it. The display case, although kept apart from probing hands by that roping and overseen by what he knew had to be guards hidden somewhere, was still awfully exposed. He had been unable to spot cameras or plainclothes cops mingling with the crowds, nor were there warning signs or obvious alarm systems. It wasn't right. There had to be something more.

The little girl bitched at her elephant.

Hawk looked up and just managed to keep his jaw from dropping.

Bingo, he thought; oh, Pope, you clever devil you. As it were, he added contritely.

A moment later a deft twitch of his hand had Pokey out of the little girl's grasp and into the air.

"These more dangerous designs," Anna continued to her charges, "inspired him to develop a secret code that—"

Pokey flew over her head.

As she turned immediately to Hawk, a brassy alarm screamed through the room, and the chandelier dropped like lead from the ceiling, inverted itself halfway down, and slammed heavily to the floor, instantly sealing the Codex display in an unassailable cage. At the same time, plumes of noxious green gas spewed from its vents.

The tourists, crying out in alarm, dashed for the staircases.

Keeping a wary eye on the progress of the gas, Hawk covered his mouth and peered through the growing cloud, noting the telltale light beams the gas illuminated—they originated in the innocuous tablets.

Pokey, alas, had been somewhat messily beheaded, a fact not unnoticed by the little girl, who screamed atrociously as she was dragged hastily away.

Anna grabbed Hawk as the green cloud approached them, and followed his gaze as he saw his two shadows helplessly trying to keep an eye on him while, at the same, escaping the gas.

"Come on," she ordered, "this stuff'll knock you out." She hurried him toward the staircase, pushing through the crowds just as two gas masks dropped from hidden beds in the arch above the entrance, allowing a pair of Vatican guards to grab them, slap them on, and fight their way down toward the Codex floor, weapons drawn. "Have you ever had the feeling you were being followed, Mr. Bond?"

"Never. Why do you ask?"

Once into the hallway, he prepared to run, but Anna nearly yanked him off his feet and through a section of the wall that had opened like a door. Inside was a narrow, ill-lighted circular staircase, its walls heavy stone and water-stained. He had no choice but to follow, and to wonder how she had known this hidden exit was here.

Nevertheless, he was impressed.

And he didn't mind the view as she preceded him toward the bottom, either.

Deeper, and darker; the air damp and clinging.

A quick glance over her shoulder. "Are you going to tell me why you did that back there, or are you going to blame it on Dumbo?"

"Oh, you mean Pokey? Hey, could you believe that crazy elephant?"

Another door easily opened, and they exited into a small underground subway, dimly lighted, the ceiling curved and stone, the walls unadorned save for a crucifix here and there. Bulging mail sacks had been stacked on the narrow platform beside the tracks, and just as he turned to watch the door close silently behind him, a tiny train pulled up, and workers popped out of the shadows to drag more loaded sacks from the open carts behind the engine.

Anna kept him back with a restraining hand.

"Hey," he said, keeping his voice low, "the Vatican IRT."

She jabbed him lightly with an elbow and pointed at the men silently hauling the sacks into place. "Delivers up to ten at night, seven days a week. Christmas cards, Easter seals . . . the Holy Father takes his mail very, very seriously. It's actually not such an unusual setup. The secret passageway, on the other hand—"

"The Vatican," Hawk recited smugly, "is made of constant mysteries meant to be enjoyed, not explained."

"Nice," she said. "But right out of our brochure."

"Oh, you read that?"

"Actually, I wrote it." She looked at him sideways. "It's a good sentence. It can apply to people."

He returned the not-unfriendly examination. "You're not an unmysterious thang yourself."

Though her lips twitched toward a smile, her eyes were somewhat skeptical. "I don't steal stuffed elephants from little girls." A quick touch to his lapels. "And my life's a little boring—"

He watched the men cart some of the bags away on squeaking hand trucks, and his face darkened. "Yeah, mine too." Then, with a shake to dispel the mood before it took hold, he brightened. "Hey, what about having a nice dull dinner with me this evening? Scrabble. Knock-knock jokes. Anecdotes about famous dead Italians."

She grinned. "I'll bring my entire repertoire."

A door opened, and he nudged her behind one of the stacks as his two Mayflower shadows spilled haplessly onto the platform. The Vatican postal workers ignored them as they began a clumsy search of the station.

Hawk tapped her on the shoulder. "And I'll bring my entourage."

She scowled at the two men, who obviously hadn't a clue what to do next. "Secret passages don't mean as much as they used to." A check to watch them move toward the other end of the platform. "There's a place two blocks east of here. Enzo's. Say ten o'clock?"

He grinned. "Said."

A quick kiss to her cheek, a sigh, and he eased away toward the nearest exit. When he was positive the flunkies weren't looking in his direction, he slipped out.

Into each miserable life, he thought, a little sunshine must fall.

Nothing was going to go wrong now.

He paused.

He frowned.

He winced, crossed his fingers quickly, and hoped that he just hadn't jinxed himself out of the first date he'd had in over a decade.

Nah, he decided then, forget it. What the hell could go wrong?

Anna watched Hawk slip away from the platform; when he was gone, her smile faded, and from the inner folds of her suit jacket, she pulled out a rosary, fussed with it, and slapped herself on the forehead.

The flunkies raced past her.

She hurried through the maze of mailbags until she reached a crucifix set into the stone wall. She looked up and cleared her throat noisily.

"Father," she said, "it's pretty obvious now. I don't know what, but he's up to something."

A speaker crackled from the vicinity of Christ's face and she winced.

"Report downstairs at once."

She nodded and left the station, not unaware of the admiring looks the workers gave her. It was, she supposed, an occupational hazard, and one she hadn't yet quite gotten used to. In a way, it was flattering; in quite another way, it was frightening.

A vigorous shake of her shoulders to drive such thoughts away, and she followed a series of narrow, dusty corridors to a large wood door that opened easily on well-oiled hinges. Waiting for her in a small room on the other side was a cardinal, his red cloak flaked with dust from the walls that appeared to be too narrow to contain him. Exits led in all directions. The only light came from naked, feeble bulbs high on the walls. He looked up when she entered, gave her a brusque nod.

"Did he mention the Mayflowers?"

No greeting. No *how are you did the gas bother you*? He waited impatiently.

She remembered her place and lowered her head. "No, Your Eminence. He's definitely going to steal the Codex. I can feel it. But I'm not sure when."

The Cardinal raised a hand imperiously. "Attempt to steal, you mean." He spat dryly. "The vanity of this man, Hudson Hawk! The Vatican has foiled the attempts of pirates and terrorists. We will not lie down for some schmuck from New Jersey!" A step forward, and the scowl deepened. "And must you flirt with him so effectively?"

She did her best not to laugh. "It's the only way, Eminence. A wise woman once said, 'Polite conversation is rarely either.'"

The Cardinal chuckled at the point well made. "Let me be the one to quote Scripture." Then he took her hands in his. "As an agent of our organization," he said, voice laced with concern, "you are put in awkward situations. Just remember, Hudson Hawk is an evil, evil man."

"Yes," she said, gently pulling herself free. "The big E."

She only wished she could sound more convincing.

12

Rome was beginning to get on Hawk's nerves. Beautiful buildings, beautiful women, beautiful food, beautiful women ... he didn't think he'd be able to stand much more without screaming, after which he'd probably be nailed by an Italian butterfly net and dragged away, never to be seen or heard of again. Tomorrow he would begin to gather the items on the list he had made while touring the Vatican. But tonight was his. Tonight he'd be with Anna, and maybe—

A clumsy sidestep around a huge fountain someone had dropped in his path, a few more awkward dance steps around the artists showing their wares at the fountain's base, and a huge grin as he continued into a glass-walled telephone booth.

A check to be sure the flunkies hadn't yet picked up his trail, and he grabbed the receiver.

Prayed.

"Yes, hello, Operator, I'd like to make a long-distance collect call to New York. Number 212-555-1898."

A moment later he whooped in silent joy when the connection was made.

The Codex, Anna, the underground station, Anna, the secret passage, Anna . . . he was right.

The telephone rang in the States.

Everything was going to be double-okay.

The telephone rang.

Still grinning, he looked idly across the teeming piazza, watching the ladies, the painters, the children, the sharklike limousine that pulled out of a shaded side street and made him dive for the booth's floor.

It's okay, he told himself, they didn't see you; it's okay, be cool, man, be cool.

"Come on, Tommy," he snapped into the receiver. "Pick up, you reindeer goat cheese-eating motherfucker!"

He kept his back to the limo.

He swore at Tommy again.

He caught a reflection of the piazza in the glass wall and knew that he hadn't seen Tommy Messina just embrace the Mayflowers and slip into their car. He knew it because Tommy was in the 5-Tone, making drinks with foam and fruit instead of boilermakers and double scotches.

"C'mon, Tommy, c'mon," he urged.

The telephone rang.

Nobody answered.

When the operator broke in to ask if he wanted to continue to hold, he snarled at her, stood, and slammed the receiver onto its cradle hard enough to shatter the earpiece. A hell of a time for Tommy to be out messing around.

The limousine drove into a crowded street, away from the piazza.

Once he was sure the limo wasn't coming back, Hawk stormed from the booth and didn't have time to duck when a tree trunk clubbed him across the chest. He fell, but instantly lashed out to catch Butterfingers square in the stomach with his heel. When the man doubled over, he leapt to his feet, grabbed the big man's head, and rammed him into into the booth's wall. Whirled to run, and stopped short with a muttered obscenity when the rest of the Candy Bars appeared out of nowhere to cut him off, expressionless, but leaving no doubt that they were carrying the means of his early demise. That none roused any attention from those in the piazza was no surprise: Snickers was in a headwaiter's outfit, and Almond Joy was a perfectly awful tourist right down to the Bermuda equally awful shorts; only Kaplan hadn't quite caught on that trench coats and stupid hats might as well have been a sign painted on his back.

Kit Kat, on the other hand, had donned a suit exactly like Hawk's. His lip even bled.

I do not want to know, Hawk decided; I do not want to know how he did that.

Kaplan took a deep breath, as if savoring the air. "Hawk, Hawk, Hawk, enjoying Italy? Y'know, I always had a soft spot for Rome. Did my first bare-handed strangulation here. Communist politician."

"Why, George," Hawk answered sourly, "you big softie."

Kaplan missed the sarcasm. "God, I miss communism. The Red Threat. People were scared, the Agency was respected, and I got laid every night."

Butterfingers waddled up, the telephone in one hand, nuggets of glass scattered across his shoulders. "Sorry, coach."

Kaplan gave Hawk a what-can-you-do? look and shook his head. "If his father wasn't the head of—" He stamped a foot, and his lips tightened. "Shit, I hate this! The government's got me farmed out, working for the Mayflower corporation now. Money beats politics. War isn't hell anymore, it's dull. Don't slaughter their men and pillage their villages, just steal their effing microchips."

Hawk wasn't moved by the tantrum. "You know, Kaplan, if you weren't the slimiest piñata of shit that ever lived, I'd feel sorry for you."

Kaplan stiffened.

Snickers glided closer. "Good news, bud—the Mayflowers have moved up the timetable. You're hitting the Vatican tonight."

Hawk spun on him in disbelief. "What? Tonight? You're whacked, man. The timing's off, I'm underequipped, and damnit, I have a date!"

Snickers shrugged. He didn't give a damn.

Almond Joy swept between them, her right hand dipping smoothly into Hawk's pocket and extracting the notebook with two fingers. When he grabbed for it, she eased away with a humorless don't-touch smile and opened it, flipped over a couple of pages and half closed one eye. "Grapple. Biker's bottle. Hair spray. Black turtleneck. Pocket fisherman. Acid. Collapsible yardstick, softball, and seventy-two stamps." The pad snapped shut. "Gee, stud, this

• 113 •

is going to be some date. No Harvey's Bristol Cream?"

Hawk wondered how a woman so lovely could be so damn ugly.

Kaplan snapped his fingers for attention. "Snickers, make the list happen." Then he pointed at Hawk. "Oh, and it's one thing to play hide-and-seek with the Mayflowers' pathetic staff, but we are sore losers. I've put jumper cables on the nipples of children, and not always in the line of duty."

Hawk knew he wasn't kidding.

Kaplan wasn't finished. "We blow up space shuttles for breakfast. You and your friend Tommy would be a late-afternoon Triscuit."

Hawk moved toward him without moving at all. "Look, jerk-off, you fuck with my friend, I'll kick all your asses."

"Yeah, right." Threats were meaningless, especially from him. He turned to leave, then turned back and smiled. "By the way, as long as I'm getting things off my chest, I'm the one who killed your little monkey. Made it look like a Mafia hit. No hard feelings. *Ciao.*"

Hawk lunged blindly, but they were gone like daylight ghosts, and all he could do was turn a tight and frustrated circle, searching for someone, anyone, to hit. "What the hell did you have against Little Eddie, you centrally intelligent scumsicle?" he yelled, not caring that he was beginning to draw stares. "Come back without your yuppie army, I'll Triscuit you, you space shuttle eating . . . shit!"

His elbow lashed out, catching Kit Kat in the face.

It felt good.

He almost smiled.

Then the man handed him a card.

Hawk looked down: *beware the blue wire.*

When he looked up, the mimic was gone and Butterfingers was in his place. No mean feat, Hawk thought.

"Hey, Mr. Hawk, I got those stamps."

Hawk took the large sheet and sighed, waved the big man away. Once again he had been too damn smart for his own good. Takes notes, why not, he grumbled to himself as he walked away; take notes, you won't forget anything, you can stall forever, what can they do?

Fathead.

He continued to grumble out of the piazza, grumbled his way through the rest of the day, and grumbled when he realized that mailing himself to the Vatican wasn't exactly the wisest trick he could have come up with. In fact, in retrospect, it was pretty dumb. More than dumb, it was dangerous. Suppose the guys who worked in the underground station decided to make a little overtime. They'd heft the package to wherever it was going, someone would open it, and someone else would be damned surprised to find a grumpy Hudson Hawk crammed inside. He didn't think wearing a skimpy bathing suit and yelling "Surprise!" would take the edge off.

But by the time he had mulled it all over and changed his mind, he had already been banged and thumped and grunted about at the post office, banged and thumped and rocked in the little train, and banged and thumped and colorfully sworn at in the station.

He held his breath.

The clock struck ten.

He counted until he was sure at least ten minutes had passed, then punched a fist through the package and waited for the alarms to go off. When they didn't, he scrambled out, gathered the pieces of the wrecked package, and stuffed them behind a stack of empty mailbags. A minute's pushing and prodding along the wall rewarded him with the secret passage Anna had shown him that afternoon. When it opened without complaining, and without setting off those alarms, he made sure his canvas bag was still hooked to his belt, then ducked inside and ran up the spiral staircase, taking the foot-worn steps two at a time until he reached the top. There, he pressed his ear against the upper door and scowled—it was too thick; he wouldn't be able to hear any of the guards.

He squinted and, with a surgeon's slow precision, opened the door.

Listened.

Poked his head out and uncrossed his fingers when he saw that the corridor was empty.

No time to waste, he reminded his reflection in one of the two mirrors flanking the Codex room entrance; you're beautiful, pal, but you're on a short fuse. He pushed his hair back with his hands, ran those same hands over the frames, and, after pulling on a pair of black gloves, nearly killed himself dragging them down from their hooks. They were even heavier than they looked, and the mirrors themselves weren't any too light either as he paused for a breath at the top of the staircase and looked out over the room. The Codex was there, caught in the beam of a soft light from the ceiling; everything else was in shadow.

His lips pursed in a congratulatory whistle and, moving as swiftly as he could with his burden, descended to the floor and set the mirrors down. He unhooked the canvas bag and opened it, took out the collapsible yardstick and gingerly set the mirrors into the top grooves so that they faced outward, the yardstick holding them together. When he was sure they wouldn't slip and fall, he pulled out the aerosol can and sprayed the air around the display case.

The light beams glowed.

Oh, yes, he thought, the man is working.

Pride goeth before destruction, a small voice quoted, and he scowled when he realized those nuns had gotten to him in more ways than one.

All right, then—save the celebrating until later.

Another spray to keep the beams in view, and he took hold of the mirrors, held his breath, and shoved them forward.

It worked: the warning beams reflected harmlessly off the glass surfaces, tricking the alarm system into thinking the light paths hadn't been broken. Next, he plunged a hand into the bag and pulled out a biker's bottle now filled with corrosive acid and crawled under the makeshift tent formed by the mirrors. Studying the case showed him several faint cracks that he immediately doused with the acid, eased back a few inches, and, as he pulled the pocket fisherman from his hip pocket, watched and grinned as the acid worked to enlarge those cracks.

A noise in the corridor startled him.

A frantic look over his shoulder showed him the shadow of a guard moving his way. If he stopped, as Hawk had done, to admire himself in the mirror, and there wasn't a mirror, and he wasn't too terribly stupid, things were going to get hectic too damn soon.

Move! he screamed silently at the acid.

The shadow spread across the corridor wall.

Please! he begged when the shadow paused.

The acid worked.

Biting hard on his lower lip, he removed the facing glass and sprayed inside, just to be sure.

And there, arced over the book, was another trap.

"Kit Kat," he whispered in admiration, "how *did* you know about the blue wire?"

He set the hook as best he could into the Codex's leather binding, then scuttled backward out from under the mirrors. There was no time to get rid of them. He extended the line and scuttled up the stairs and behind a pedestal holding an unnamed saint's imposing statue. He didn't look at it; guilt was something he didn't need right now.

The shadow spread ominously onto the stairs, and a guard whose bulk reminded him of Big Stan back in New York rushed down the stairs, skidding and slipping to a halt when he spotted the mirrors. He bent over. He gasped when he saw the acid dripping onto the floor.

Don't look, Hawk ordered.

The guard looked at the wire.

Damn.

Hawk leapt from behind the statue and yanked the wire.

The guard turned.

The Codex flew from its perch and landed neatly in Hawk's arms.

It wasn't until then that all hell broke loose.

13

For the briefest of moments, but no longer than that because he was a good man but not a complete idiot, Hawk felt sorry for the bumbling Italian version of Big Stan. The poor slob was trapped in the cage that had plummeted down from the ceiling and was now flailing about helplessly as the green knockout gas billowed into the room. Hawk immediately plucked a softball from his bag and threw it at one of the windows on the other side of the room.

At the same time, two more guards charged onto the landing, but this time only one gas mask dropped from its bed. One guard was quick; the other one crumpled slowly to the floor.

Life, Hawk told the fallen man, is tough, ain't it.

As the second guard hurried down the steps toward the display, Hawk let out a length of high-tensile cord into a loop, spun it and the attached grapple over his head several times, then launched it at the thick chain that held the chandelier/cage.

When it caught, he grabbed it as high as he could, took a breath, closed his eyes, and jumped.

The trajectory swung him easily over the head of the guard, over the cage, and onto the opposite staircase, almost directly in front of the window the softball had shattered. Eat your heart out, Tarzan, he thought; a deft snap of his wrist then, and the grapple came loose, whipping toward him and landing with a clang at his feet.

The guard in the gas mask heard the noise and came running, one hand on his still-holstered gun.

Hawk gathered up the line-and-grapple and leapt through the window, sprawled onto a ledge, and told himself not to look down.

He did.

He swallowed heavily.

Dead people are down there, he thought; they were alive when they were up here, but when they landed down there, they got dead.

He shuddered and tore off the gas mask, pushed himself to his feet and started across the roof, which, he realized glumly, would have been a lot easier to manage if it had been flat.

It wasn't.

It was slanted, it was tile and slate, and it was slippery as melted butter.

All I need now is a little rain, he thought, then looked quickly heavenward; sorry, only kidding.

Please.

Glass crunched and cracked behind him; the guard was out on the roof.

He doubled his speed and, just before he fell, told himself it wasn't a good idea to hurry.

He only skidded a few feet before catching himself with hands pressed hard to the slate, but the canvas bag, and the Codex inside, slid inexorably down toward the gutter. He watched it helplessly, and almost cheered his good fortune when it caught on the base of a canted television antenna.

Inside, the Pope, still wearing his skullcap but exchanging his daytime ceremonial robes for a Notre Dame bathrobe, scowled at his television. Just when Mr. Ed was explaining something vital to the human race to that numbskull, Wilbur, the picture had gone all fuzzy.

He grumbled.

Waddled over to the set.

Slammed it with his fist and dared it not to work.

The guard yelled at Hawk to stop.

In another life maybe, he answered silently, and hooked the grapple onto the narrow, reasonably flat peak of the roof and let himself slide down. He refused to think about how exposed he was this way, and refused to think about what would happen if the grapple came loose. That antenna didn't look as if it would hold the weight of a full-grown falling man.

The line came up short.

The guard fired, missing wildly.

Hawk swore at the bag and reached toward it.

The guard fired again.

Hawk looked just beyond the bag to the distance he would fall if his luck turned more sour than it already had. "Please, God," he gasped, his fingers brushing the bag's handle. "Please, God, let the guard shoot me."

The guard fired.

Never mind!

He grabbed the bag and began to haul himself back up, his soles sliding on the tiles, the bag hindering his grip on the sweat-slick cord.

Evidently realizing that his marksmanship left a whole lot to be desired, the guard climbed onto the flat peak and made his way gingerly toward the grapple.

Hawk froze, perspiration beginning to break across his forehead and under his arms.

It was too late.

The guard grinned down at him, hitched up his belt, and took a sliding step forward. "The worm's on the other foot, Yankee Doodle Candy."

He chuckled and slid forward again.

Hawk braced himself and yanked the cord, whipping it against the man's ankle and spilling him backward off the peak with a surprised, terrified yell. Hawk didn't take the time to find out what happened; he hauled himself to the top, snatched up the grapple, and ran as fast as he could, one arm out for balance, his eyes focused straight ahead, to the end of the roof and a low brick wall that rose a few feet above it. He didn't know what was on the other side. He didn't care. Anyplace, now, was better than this.

A gunshot.

He looked back and saw the guard pulling himself hand over hand back toward the peak, trying to take aim and climb at the same time.

Amazing, he thought, they get paid enough to do this?

Nimbly he leapt atop the wall and spun the grapple's rope again, released it and yanked it humming taut when it tumbled into the branches of a wide-crowned tree on the other side of the road. Before the rope had stopped quivering, he tied his end off on a broken section of the wall, grabbed a wide friction belt from inside the bag, and looped it over the cord.

He looked down.

He looked back as the guard struggled to his knees on the peak.

I am blessed, he thought, to know such brave men.

Then: "Jesus!" when the guard fired a wild shot.

He jumped.

The wind of his passage deafened him, and he suddenly realized that he hadn't figured out how he would stop one of the branches from impaling him.

It didn't matter.

Another shot that he heard all too clearly, and the friction belt parted.

He yelled as he fell, yelled again when he landed astride a fork-topped street lamp and gripped it tightly, gasping at the pain, wondering painfully if this meant he would never have to worry about paying for a kid's wedding or college education; whatever else, his love life was definitely stuck on hold for a while.

It was too much.

His hands wouldn't maintain their grip, and he fell again, this time with resignation, this time not making a sound when he landed on a fast-moving bus piled high with luggage, and flimsy crates filled with chickens, lashed on the roof. His eyes watering with agony, he tried to stand up, to see if the guard had made it to the wall, but the bus suddenly swerved around a corner without slowing, and he was flung off.

I *hate* my name, he thought, pinwheeled, and landed square on a chair that rocked, trembled, but didn't collapse.

Am I dead yet?

He wiped his face and looked around.

No; he was in a sidewalk café, and the few other patrons were staring at him, dumbfounded.

Then he looked across the table and decided that either someone really had it in for him, or someone really thought he deserved another chance.

Anna lowered her menu and smiled relief. "Hawk! I was worried you weren't going to drop by."

A quick adjustment of his clothes, his hair, and a press against his chest to be sure his heart was still where it belonged, and he smiled as he set the bag snugly in his lap and patted it thankfully.

"Am I late?" Easy, he told himself then, be cool.

He blew a chicken feather out of his mouth.

"You look really nice." Good. Nicely put, you jerk. "Did I really say nice?"

A waiter interrupted then, saved him with a request for their order.

"Fettucini con Funghi Porcini, prego," Hawk said with a debonair flip of his hand.

Anna smiled her admiration.

"Bellissimo, signore."

Hawk agreed, whatever the man said. "Oh, and could I have some ketchup with that?"

Anna slapped her forehead with the heel of her

hand, and the waiter slouched away with head lowered, so clearly disenchanted that Hawk almost called him back. This guilt stuff, he thought, was getting to be a pain. He wondered if waiters took classes in it.

Several yards and tables distant, Snickers squirmed in his seat and looked away from Hawk, and the woman at the table with him. He didn't like the way the burglar looked at his date, and he was damn sure Kaplan wasn't going to like it either.

A snort of disgust.

He glared at their stoic waiter, and at the hapless Butterfingers, who was trying, none too successfully, to make himself understood.

"Come on, Pierre," the big man pleaded, "steak burger. Steak. Burg. Er. Frennnnnch friiiiiiies." He looked around in disgust, wondering what was wrong. "This is France. You gotta have French, right?"

Almond Joy patted his hand to get his attention. "Actually, we're in Italy, Butterfingers."

He looked at her.

She smiled warmly.

Snickers didn't bother to stop the waiter when he took the moment to disappear. In a hurry.

"Hell," he complained when they were alone. "Italy, France, Moscow, they all just want to be Nebraska. Old Man Kaplan thinks since communism is dead, we got nothing to do. Man, democracy isn't free elections." He stared at each of them in turn. "We got to teach the world that democracy is big tits, college football on Saturdays, Eddie Murphy saying 'fuck,' and kids putting their hands down garbage disposals on *America's Funniest Home Videos*."

Almond Joy shook her head in sympathy. "Damn, baby, when's the last time you had a vacation?" She leaned back and clawed her hands through her hair, massaged the back of her neck, and groaned. "Jesus, I gotta get out of this job, y'know? If my mom knew her only daughter had assassinated the leader of an anti-apartheid movement—"

"Oh, quit bitching," Snickers snarled. "You get the Employee of the Month plaque for that shit, you know."

Butterfingers's knuckles thumped the table lightly to shut them up, remind them why they were here. When they all looked back to Hawk's table, he sighed and said, "Ah to be in Paris and in love."

Hawk knew he wasn't the most suave man in the world, probably not even in the top hundred as such things were measured, but he damn sure knew blatant sarcasm when he saw it. Which he did when the waiter returned with a large straw basket in which was nestled a ketchup bottle wrapped in a clean white towel. He offered it with a slight bow.

Hawk accepted the bottle and smiled the man's dismissal. "This," he declared as he examined the label, "is buono. I tell you, they had the worst damn ketchup in prison that . . ." He sniffed. He looked at Anna. "Uh."

Anna's smile was tentative. "Prison?"

"The warden!" Hawk countered quickly. "I was the warden." And groaned inwardly when he realized that not only didn't she buy it, she hadn't even looked in the window.

But neither, he noted, was she repulsed.

"How . . . how long were you in?"

Deny, lie, or out with it.

Damn, he hated these ethical decisions.

"Let's just say I never saw *E.T.*"

Her mouth opened, closed, and she folded her hands under her chin. "Wow, you were in the joint. Doing hard time." Her lips parted slowly. "It's funny, but that excites me. I seem to have a thing for sinners."

The nuns, he thought, are never going to believe this.

"And I," he answered, "have a thing for sinning. Check, please!"

The waiter floated over and glanced at the table, and the uneaten food on both their plates. His expression didn't change. "Anything for dessert?"

Anna's eyes half closed as she looked straight at Hawk. "Yes. Something to go."

Hawk waggled his eyebrows. "Great," he said. "I'll bring the ketchup."

He stood instantly, grabbed the canvas bag before it hit the ground, and decided that Mayflower could wait for his damn book.

Ten years.

Ten *long* years.

And that goddamn Bunny was nowhere in sight.

14

It was a small apartment not far from the café, fairly Spartan in its furnishings, which surprised Hawk a little considering how understatedly glamorous Anna was. Despite the fact that she was, after all, a doctor of something or other, and that she did work for the Vatican in some advisory capacity or other, he still expected a bit more than just a few simple pieces of furniture and a few clearly inexpensive prints on the walls. Maybe it was because he was still in his Sing Sing decor mode, where the most the inmates could come up with were generally cutouts from *Playboy* and calendars from tire companies, except, of course, for the guy on the level below his who seemed to have a thing for pictures of hedges. He had never asked why. After the first year, he hadn't wanted to know.

At any rate, aside from a scattering of scholarly texts, coffee-table art books big enough to fell a horse, and the prints and replica statuary, there was nothing he could see that would tell him who or what she was.

But her bed was something else again. Gleaming brass headboard, thick mattress just soft enough to sink into without breaking your back, pillows to drown in, and clean. Lord, it was clean.

He sighed.

Facedown, his jacket and shirt off, he wriggled his shoulders into the crisp sheets, smelled the soap, and smelled *her*. It was, so far, the best thing that had happened to him since his first breath of free air.

He stretched and relaxed, wriggled again, and swallowed a sigh. His eyes were half-closed, his mouth open in ecstasy as a barefoot Anna straddled him without crushing him and massaged his back, expertly, with hands surprisingly strong. Every few seconds she would stop, and he groaned a plea that made her giggle and start all over again.

When she broke the silence at last, her voice was quiet, not quite calm: "Why do they call you Hudson Hawk?"

He thought about it, considered several perfectly wonderful, and very romantic, lies, until he remembered that, despite it all, he was supposed to be going straight.

"The hawk," he said, "is a slang word for the wind that blows in the winter. I grew up in a town called Hoboken, in New Jersey. Well, Hoboken is on the Hudson River. So . . . Hudson Hawk."

A moment.

Then, even softer: "So why do they call you Hawk?"

Her fingers flexed and rubbed.

He sighed. "Anytime anybody needed something stolen—needed a favor, that is—they'd come to me and I'd perform that favor like a hawk. You know, like the wind."

As she worked on, he could sense her examination of his back, and eventually, inevitably, she remarked on the curious number of bruises she found.

"Where did you get these?"

He chuckled, turned his head onto his right cheek, and looked out the curtained window, at the flickering lights of the city, the matching lights of the night sky. Traffic was little more than a murmur. Occasional voices little more than dreams. Despite the lechery in his veins, he was close to dozing off, and started when she asked him again how he'd managed to bang his back up so badly. Without moving his head, he looked back and up. "I had a little accident around the house."

"What happened?"

"I fell on some chickens."

"Does it hurt?"

"Yes, it hurts."

"Maybe I can make them better."

Oh, boy, he thought.

"See what you can do. Just don't tickle."

He shifted, waited, sensed her leaning closer, could feel her breath drift like a summer breeze across his skin. Moist. Warm. His eyes closed all the way, waiting for the feel of her lips on his back, the signal that the chase would soon begin in earnest.

She tickled him.

"Hey! That tickles!"

She tickled him again, moving around his waist expertly, sadistically.

"Tickles!" he yelled, beginning to laugh and hating himself for it.

She wouldn't let up.

"Tickles!" he bellowed in case she'd suddenly lost the ability to understand English.

But she didn't stop, and his laughter bucked him, rolled him over to retaliate, and they were quickly wrestling across the mattress, fighting for the upper hand and laughing so hard they didn't feel a thing when they finally spilled off the mattress onto the floor.

He wasted no time.

Choking back the echoes of more laughter, he crawled around to her feet and began to nibble at her toes. He had heard it was still sexy; he had heard women loved this sort of thing; he had heard that women who lived alone in simple apartments in Rome were animals when it came to having their toes done.

He glanced up along her shadowed body to see how she was taking it.

He grinned.

He watched her back arch, watched her hands grasp at the air, watched her freeze when she spotted the crucifix on the wall, watched himself add another damn day to those already long days already added to those damn ten years.

Gently, but firmly, she pushed him away and used the edge of the bed to pull herself shakily to her feet. "I'm sorry." Her face was flushed; she seemed ready to weep. "I can't do this."

All right, no big deal. He'd just gone a little too

fast, that's all. He had been deprived, and doctor types who spend their days writing tourist brochures and examining books with more dust than words are probably a little skittish. Nothing to worry about. Slow and steady wins the race; remember what the ant did to that rubber tree plant.

He stood and moved toward her, hoping his smile was more understanding than lecherous. "Hey now," he said quietly, "outside of a very friendly dog this morning, it's been a slow decade. I don't make love every ten years, I tend to get a little cranky."

Flustered, she held out her hands to fend him off and ended up gripping his arms lightly. He could feel her trembling. "It's ... it's also been a long time for me. I—"

He leaned closer.

Her lips parted.

The crucifix began shrieking in Italian.

Hawk leapt away with a terrified yelp, looking for somewhere to hide from the lightning that just had to be streaking across the city toward his skull. "Man, Catholic girls are scary," he said when Anna turned to the cross and cocked her head.

She looked over her shoulder, hushing him with a finger. After a second outburst, she clasped her hands and said, "Somebody robbed the Vatican."

"Oh," Hawk said. "No."

As soon as the crucifix quieted, she grabbed her shoes and slipped them on as she hopped across the bedroom floor, babbling something he couldn't understand. In the front room she headed directly for the door, and he gasped when he realized that her lurching side to side was going to knock his canvas bag off the side table by the couch.

He lunged to intercept her.

She tripped and stumbled against the table.

The bag turned over, opened, and the Codex flew out.

He lunged again, this time for the book, and they both managed to get a hand on it.

She looked at it, eyes wide in disbelief.

He looked at it, thinking it looked a hell of a lot older in here than back in its case, and that there was no way in hell he was going to talk his way out of this one.

She looked at him, aghast.

He wondered where the hell his nimble wit and quick tongue were now, now that he needed them.

She didn't give him a chance. She yanked the ancient book from his grasp and ran for the door, but his recovery was too quick, and he came up behind her in a single long stride, grabbed her around the waist, and pulled her back into his chest.

The book fell.

She glared at him as she tried to twist out and away.

"Hey, it's not what you think." Good, Hawk, really clever. "Okay, maybe it is."

Her struggle intensified, but at the last he was too strong. "You did it!" she yelled. "You really went and did it!" She stopped, turned in the circle of his arm, and stared at him incredulously. "With one day, not even a day of planning, you did it." She shook her head in reluctant admiration. "Nobody does it better, Hudson. You started the week stealing the 'Sforza' and ended it by stealing da Vinci's Codex.''

"What?''

"So what are your plans for the weekend? Hoisting the Colosseum? Tell me, did the devil make you do it, or was it Darwin and Minerva Mayflower?''

The street below the apartment building was dark, street lamps buried in foliage. The shops were closed. A motorcycle growled through an intersection. Beneath a somewhat ragged tree, a car waited at the curb. Inside, Snickers, crammed into the front seat with his two cohorts, tried to slam a cartridge into his revolver. Butterfingers worked on an Italian pastry that more often than not landed on his chest instead of his mouth.

"Dunkin's better,'' the big man finally declared, defeated, and wiped his hands on his pants.

Almond Joy tried to look across the street and up to a window where two shadows moved back and forth behind a curtain. "What's going on in there?''

Butterfingers belched. "Do you want me to rape them?''

Snickers rolled his eyes. "Just go read, okay?''

The big man nodded agreeably and pulled a thin green book from the dashboard, a biography of Leonardo da Vinci, written by Dr. Anna Baragli. He opened it to a dog-eared page and squinted in the dim light.

" 'Da Vinci had fears about his more dangerous designs, so he created a shorthand code in reverse script—' ''

"To yourself!'' Almond Joy snapped. And: "What the *hell* are they doing up there?''

Butterfingers grumbled about not getting his education, and she slapped the book from his hands.

"Jesus, enough, for God's sake!" Snickers growled. "Twenty seconds, and we go in."

Hawk was astonished, but not really surprised, at how complicated the world had become since his dear, dear friend Kaplan had sent him away. For example: in older times, when a woman discovered he had stolen one of the world's most valuable treasures, she would have screamed bloody murder, called the cops, and promptly found something to disembowel him with. Most likely, her bare hands. Anna, on the other hand, plopped him down in a chair and pulled a beaded curtain away from her kitchen alcove. There, gloriously and will miracles never cease, was a cappuccino machine that she worked as if she used it every day.

Admiration blossomed.

Lust took a temporary stroll around the block when she turned from her ministrations at the counter and presented him with a perfectly foamed cup of his elixir of life.

Heaven, and an angel too, he thought; maybe the nuns were wrong, after all.

"You see," she explained as he blew the foam gently, teasing himself and loving it, "for two years I've been tracking the Mayflowers' peculiar interest in three da Vinci pieces. Their 'Sforza' replica was as fake as the so-called gas leak that supposedly destroyed it."

He shook his head. "Does everybody in the world know more than me? Jesus, I'm just some guy who happens to be good at swiping stuff." He grinned at her. " 'Hey, Dad, can you tell me what time it is?' 'Sure, son—whoa, wait a minute, who took my watch? Oh, you got me again, boy.' " He held his cup up in an unspoken toast. "Who knew it would lead to this? They even got the CIA involved."

"What?" she said loudly. "The CIA? What are you—"

"Well, well, well." He looked at her over the top of the cup. "I guess I do know something after all. Here's looking at you, kid."

She said nothing.

At last, he thought as he brought the cup to his lips; all this time, all this trouble, all this shooting and running and hiding, and I finally get my reward.

He raised an eyebrow at her.

She said nothing.

He shrugged, and sipped.

He made a face and felt a tingling begin to spread along the inside of his mouth.

He looked at the machine, at Anna, at the cup. "You know, I don't want to be rude, but this sure doesn't taste like the cappuccino I used to know."

The tingling intensified, began to seep into his veins, his limbs, curl around the corners of his mind.

Well, I'll be damned, he thought as he pushed himself to his feet, trying to move quickly and finding his legs suddenly transformed into lead, which was all right this time since someone had glued his feet to the floor.

Anna picked up a thick pillow from the couch and tossed it onto the carpet. "Nuts, I must have put too much ethyl chloride in it."

Of course you did, he said, though his lips didn't move; and you're going to pay for this, lady, as soon as I sleep for three or four years.

His knees buckled and gave way; she plucked the cup neatly from his hand and placed it on the table, then cupped the back of his head and followed him down until he was stretched out on the floor, staring at the ceiling and watching the room begin to fade into night.

He didn't blink when she kissed his cheek; he didn't start when the door smashed in off its hinges and Butterfingers fell atop it; he didn't groan when the other Candy Bars charged in over him, guns high and ready; he didn't do much of anything when Anna turned on them angrily.

"Why didn't you tell me at the restaurant that he'd hit the Vatican tonight? My people will not be happy." She glared down at him, then pointed at Snickers. "I want to see Kaplan."

Oh, my, Hawk thought, floating somewhere far away and not giving a damn, oh, my.

"That's not overly possible," Almond Joy answered.

"For security reasons," Snickers clarified as he tucked his gun away, "Mr. Kaplan's coordinates are being kept secret even from us."

My, Hawk thought, and good night, all.

"But, guys," Butterfingers said from his place on the fallen door, "he's at the castle in Vinci."

My, Hawk thought again, and prayed they wouldn't put him back in the trunk.

After several minutes of heated arguing over the relative merits of dragging versus lifting, and why not just shoot him and be done with it, for Pete's sake, Butterfingers slung him effortlessly over his shoulder with one hand and carried him down the stairs. His head thumped the wall a few times, and the big man wasn't too careful about dumping him into the back of a car that smelled like a bakery, but Hawk couldn't hang on to consciousness much longer to really give a damn. He faded in and out, hearing but not understanding anything the others said, feeling the car swerve and jerk through evening traffic until the lights stopped flashing and he realized they were somewhere beyond the city.

The car stopped.

He was lifted out and carried across what he assumed was a field.

His vision blurred.

He heard someone say something about his falling out—accidentally, of course—and then they wouldn't have any more trouble with the son of a bitch.

The last thing he saw was the helicopter.

The last thing he heard was someone else saying with a giggle that he hoped the hawk could fly.

15

It occurred to Hawk as the helicopter swooped sickeningly over a low hill not long after dawn that he was getting awfully good at not quite dying, a skill for which he supposed he ought to be extremely grateful. Ordinarily he preferred to avoid excitement. It was bad for the heart, bad for sober thinking, and bad for his future. This, however, was getting ridiculous.

Nevertheless, still groggy from the mickey Anna had slipped him, and still trying to decide just whose side she was on, he couldn't help a slight widening of the eyes when he saw the castle in the distance. A real castle. A fairy princess castle. And the closer they flew, the wider his eyes grew. It was amazing. He didn't think things like that existed in real life outside of Disneyland.

Then the aircraft banked, all he saw was the ground, and his stomach suggested he either close his eyes now, or lose it.

He closed his eyes.

He drifted off despite all efforts to remain conscious, and only felt himself being carried into the cool morning air, footsteps hard on the ground, then on stone, then echoing in what could only be a stone corridor. Up several flights of stairs, around several corners, and a jolt of nausea when Butterfingers dumped him without warning into a high-backed wood chair. He swallowed several times before opening his eyes, didn't shake his head out of respect for his still-protesting stomach, and frowned his puzzlement.

The room was dark in spite of the dawn's glow in the window. It was some sort of workshop or study—drafting tables of unknown age, a desk, empty bookshelves, and over in the corner an easel minus its canvas. There were too many shadows for him to make out exactly what was on each surface, but when Butterfingers stepped aside, a few of the shadows finally moved.

One of them coalesced into Anna, who, after an initial glance in his direction, steadfastly refused to meet his gaze, which, under the circumstances, he considered a good sign. She was guilty. It was plastered all over her, and if he could only stop his head from spinning and his mind from buzzing, he might be able to figure out exactly why.

Kaplan, who obviously owned only one set of clothes, gestured toward Hawk. "Way to go, Anna." Then he crossed to a small table on which lay the Codex. "The Mayflowers are going to try to make a deal for this, and then we'll bust those greedy pigs. Operation Deflower Mayflower."

She held up a cautionary finger. "Before we break out the little lollipops, I should tell you that Hudson . . . Mr. Hawk . . . Hawkins here had some pretty neat things to say about Darwin, Minerva, and you." She glanced around the room. "Basically, that you're all part of the same car pool."

"Oh?" Kaplan said with exaggerated disappointment. A chiding shake of his head. "Anna, Anna, Anna. If that was true, Almond Joy here would have handed you your heart right after you handed me the Codex." A forgive-and-forget smile. "Now get some sleep, okay? Kit Kat . . . ?"

Kit Kat, dressed in the same blouse and skirt Anna wore, glided up beside her. She looked at him strangely. "Cat got his tongue?"

"Actually, he never told us what it was. *Arrivederci*, baby."

When Kit Kat smiled broadly, and deliberately slowly, Hawk could see that he indeed had no tongue, and he squirmed uneasily in his seat. Then he tried to tell Anna with a look as she left how miserable he was, how hurt he was, how confused he was. The return look as she slipped out of the door only confirmed his impression that she was, for whatever reason, feeling awfully damned guilty about something. Something more than ruining his cappuccino.

The door closed.

He scrubbed his cheeks with his palms, put knuckles to his eyes to clear them.

"With all due respect to that great blouse," Almond Joy said to her boss, "why didn't I tear out her heart?"

Kaplan picked up the Codex. "Close call, but she's our only way of keeping tabs on that damn mysterious Vatican organization. They have no idea that Operation Deflower Mayflower is as bogus as Kit Kat's tits." He moved across the room and held out his hand to pull Hawk to his feet. "Time to go to the principal's office, old friend."

It would have been a great time to attempt an escape if it hadn't been for the armament the Candy Bars were carrying, and the fact that his legs still felt wobbly. So Hawk simply nodded and, learning that his legs were finally working again, followed Kaplan out of the workshop into a dark, dusty corridor. More stairs, more turns, and at last into a virtual cavern of a room that made him pause until Snickers jabbed a finger into his back. He moved on without complaint, keeping to the perimeter where billowing sheets covered things too large to be simply furniture. At the far end was an automatic tennis-ball machine, and the Mayflowers in what he supposed were today's idea of spiffy court clothes—Darwin was with racket, Minerva was on a lounge with a remote control that spat out the balls, and Alfred was in sweat togs, retrieving.

Hawk kept his mouth shut.

Minerva buttoned, Darwin swung, the ball slammed off two walls and into Alfred's forehead.

"Jolly. Good. Shot. Sir," the butler assassin managed.

Minerva looked away from her husband, and smiled. "Oh, it's Hudson Hawk!" The smile vanished. "You never cease to amaze me, convict. You are one terrible cat burglar."

Darwin swatted another one, his form careless. Alfred ducked. "Haven't you ever seen like David Niven, Hawk? You know, tiptoe in, tiptoe out?"

"Like a cat, one could say," Minerva added.

Hawk wasn't amused. "Well, hell, I'll just take it back and do it all over."

No one laughed.

He reached for the Codex snuggled under Kaplan's arm, but the trench coat ignored him, moving smoothly out of his way to meet Darwin in the middle of the room. Mayflower blew a welcoming kiss to the priceless tome, then split the binding and pulled out a crystal, held it up to the light.

It flared as if trapping lasers in its core.

"Ah," Hawk said before he could stop himself, "another piece of the puzzle for the da Vinci Alchemy Project."

When the others looked at him, looked at each other, and began to demand just how the hell he knew about that, he slapped himself mentally a few times and hoped he hadn't pulled the coffin lid over himself this time. One of these days he was going to learn.

Kaplan, unhappy and not caring who knew it, took a menacing step toward him, but was forestalled when the two flunkies who'd been tailing Hawk through the Vatican rushed into the room. Nervous. Close to frightened.

"Oh, you," said Darwin. He tsked. "There's nothing I hate more than failure. All you had to do was follow the Hawk. It's not like I ordered you to teach the nation's children to read, you know." He sighed heavily. "I guess we're just going to have to kill them."

Hawk would have laughed, but without missing a beat, Minerva pulled a small gun from beneath her whites and shot the two men. Between the eyes.

The walls and floor speckled red long before they fell.

Jesus, Hawk thought, and sidled away.

"God, Minerva," Darwin said, "I was only kidding."

She shrugged.

They laughed.

Hawk kept moving. They may act like clowns, they may be on the far side of nuts, but they were deadly, and he needed something, anything, to give him an edge. A cannon would do in a pinch, but he doubted he'd be so lucky. As the others fussed over the bodies, he touched at the sheets, trying to guess what was beneath them. Something poked his back sharply. He spun around to see what he'd done, saw another covering, this one on a forklift, and snapped out his hand when a small object slithered free. He caught it, looked down, and frowned when he saw a gold demon's head in his palm.

"Get away from there, convict!" Minerva yelled.

He backed away quickly, the demon's head palmed. "Just browsing. Don't touch me."

Snickers eased up and touched him.

That, thought Hawk, does it.

The sound of his fist meeting the young man's pointed jaw was satisfying enough to make him forget how hard a man's jaw was, pointed or not, and how badly knuckles tended to ache after a punch. But it was fun, and when Snickers recovered and came at him, he was ready for an encore.

"No!" Darwin commanded. "Don't hurt him. We need him for the final job."

Hawk knew he shouldn't be thinking what he was thinking, and he knew that he was going to get into a major conflict here, but he simply couldn't resist. He'd been battered, drugged, dragged, lied to, and blackmailed. This was too good to pass up.

"Really?" he said innocently. "Don't hurt me?"

Snickers snarled at him in frustration.

Hawk realized that a true adult would not yield unto the temptation that had been placed before him.

"You mean," he said, yielding, "even if I do this?" He pulled Snickers's glasses off and stomped on them, then ground their lenses with his heel.

Snickers trembled with helpless indignation.

Hawk, giddy with power, moseyed over to Butterfingers. "And this?" A knee to the big man's stomach doubled him over. "Surely, now, this must offend." And he slammed into Butterfingers just hard enough to catapult him into Snickers and send them both to the floor.

He grinned.

He shadowboxed a little and swung in front of Alfred, whose expression didn't change when his arm raised and the too-familiar, very long knife glittered in the room's gold light.

Hawk put on the brakes and lost the smile.

Alfred stared at him.

"Come to think of it," Minerva said, "there is a part of your body you're not going to need for your next job."

Hawk turned on her angrily. "Damnit, I'm involved in this thing, so I just want to know what this thing is. I want to be treated as an adult."

Silence.

Snickers hissing then, and Butterfingers groaning.

The *snick* of Alfred's blade sliding back into its sheath.

Darwin scratched the back of his neck, looked to Kaplan and his wife, and finally threw up his hands. "All right," he agreed. "That's fair. But tomorrow. Back in Rome."

Hawk nodded.

Darwin smiled. "Fine. Now go to your room."

Hawk was about to ask where that might be, and if the princess of the castle was included, when Alfred grabbed him where his shoulder met his neck.

Squeezed.

And Hawk blacked out.

Anna sat in the musty, cramped confessional booth, thinking about Hawk and the trouble she'd gotten him into, and the trouble she was going to get him into if things didn't clear up pretty soon. Which they wouldn't. That kind of future wasn't in his cards.

She sighed.

She heard the Cardinal settling himself noisily in the other side and wished he'd hurry up. Matters were boiling to a head and the longer she stayed away, the more danger Hawk was in.

"Forgive me, Father, for I have sinned," she said when she sensed he was ready. "It's been twelve hundred hours since my last confession."

A silence, and she thought for a moment she heard the Cardinal yawn.

"All right," he said in resignation, "hit me with your best shot."

Anna took a slow breath. "I betrayed a man. A good man. An innocent man . . . a thief."

The Cardinal cleared his throat. "Anna, what are you trying to say?"

Be strong, she cautioned herself, he's not going to like this.

"He came into a world where crime is a legitimate business tactic and a legitimate government procedure. But he knew Right from Wrong." Another breath. "Oh, and we kind of messed around a little."

She winced when he exploded into such rapid-fire Italian that she could only understand one word in twenty. When he finally returned to English, it wasn't much better.

"Messed around? You mean messed around messed around? I knew—I don't want to know. What? First base? Second base? Stop me when I'm getting warm."

She bridled. "A little petting is not the issue!"

A brief silence.

An apologetic sigh. "Sorry. Seventeen Hail Marys and five minutes outside."

She covered her face, blew out in relief, and pushed aside the heavy curtain. When she stepped out of the booth she fussed a bit with the nun's habit she wore, adjusted the wimple, and smiled broadly at the Cardinal, who was clearly not amused.

"So, Sister," he said grimly, "what you are saying is that Hudson Hawk is not willingly working for the Mayflowers, but Kaplan and the Candy Bars are?"

She nodded as they walked away, Cardinal and nun, the church around them stunning in its hushed, reverent beauty, inspiring in its elegance.

Her habit rustled quietly as she moved beside her mentor and superior, and she wondered what Hawk would think if he ever learned the truth. She knew he would absolutely hate the black clunker shoes.

"You got it," she answered when the Cardinal repeated his assessment. "Operation Deflower Mayflower is a joke. And I'm the punch line." She glanced at him angrily. "I thought we were using the CIA to help us get Mayflower, but they're really using me to keep us *away* from him."

The Cardinal wrung his hands and shook his head, looked up at a solemn-faced saint and shook his head again. "Why couldn't I just be the Cardinal in charge of catering? But not me. Oh, no." He swung into the center aisle and headed for the exit, Anna hurrying to keep pace. "If the Mayflowers get the three sections of da Vinci's crystal and his instructions for the gold machine . . ." He pressed the heels of his hands against his temples. "Do we got anything? What of Tommy 5-Tone, Hawk's friend? Where is his loyalty?"

Anna admitted she didn't know. "But I'm going to find out."

At the door, the Cardinal took her hand and smiled contritely. "I'm sorry for losing it back there, Sister, but you must remember that you have vows to God as well as a mission to the world."

Tell me about me, she thought sourly.

"I know, I know, Your Eminence," she said aloud. "Just say God go with me."

His smile softened. "God go with you, Sister."

Right, she thought; and boy, am I going to need it.

From the folds of her habit she pulled an extravagant pair of sunglasses, slipped them on as the Cardinal opened the heavy door, and waved at him as she stepped into the light.

When the door closed, her shoulders sagged and her legs felt momentarily weak.

Hawk, she prayed as she hurried down the steps, keep your head up. If you think it's bad now, just wait a few minutes.

16

For a change, Hawk was glad he couldn't see anything. He wouldn't have to endure the Mayflower Building, the conference room, and especially that god-awful portrait of the Mayflowers that hung like a garish vulture over the M-shaped conference room. As it was, he had already shuddered as if dipped in ice when Alfred guided him in and dropped him unceremoniously in a chair, and he nearly embraced the man when the blindfold went on. The artery squeeze that had blacked him out was forgiven for the time being; after all, the guy was only doing his job.

And one of these days, when this nightmare was over and he was able to look over his shoulder without seeing half the world's spies, creeps, and psychos sneaking around after him, he was going to take that smarmy butler's goddamn knife and carve him a new, unsmiling mouth, somewhere in the vicinity of the underside of his jaw.

A careful touch on his shoulder; a reminder to be good.

On the other hand, Hawk thought, maybe I'll just let it go, be generous, live to a ripe old age.

A faint murmur of voices suggested that the board members had filed into the room and were taking their seats.

The sound of a whooping siren deep in the city.

He shifted uncomfortably, willed his hands away from the blindfold, and wondered what his captors had in store for him now. The Bank of England? Fort Knox? Mars? After the Vatican job, places like that ought to be a piece of cake.

He listened for a sign of further activity, but heard nothing; there was, for the moment, silence, although he thought he detected the little old lady wheezing.

The silence lengthened.

Somebody coughed discreetly.

A padded footstep behind him, and fading.

Then silence.

His nerves began to stretch.

He shifted again and tried to think of something else. Throughout the previous night and the long trip back to Rome he had tried to decipher the puzzle of the crystal and what Anna's part was in this elaborate charade. She wasn't, he knew instinctively, one of the bad guys. Mayflower was a bad guy; Kaplan and his cronies were bad guys; Cesar Mario was stupid and bad, and pretty dead.

But not Anna.

He refused to believe that the Vatican would hook up with any of the people thus far involved, despite its obvious strong interest in the Project. The Alchemy Project. Whatever the hell that was.

So who was she? Really?

And why, if she was honestly attracted to him, hadn't she been more responsive? Not even a kiss, for crying out loud. It was unnatural. He wasn't *that* ugly, was he? His past was shady, but nothing like Officer Gates. Could it be that he—

A finger prodded his shoulder—another reminder, this time to pay attention.

He cocked his head as he heard someone pacing about the room, then frowned when Alfred of the cold fingers positioned his hands on the table's cool surface. Not long afterward, something heavy was placed on each palm. His fingers curled automatically around them.

Mayflower cleared his throat theatrically. "So, Captain Hawk, in one of your paws you have a gold bar worth about eight thousand. In the *autre*, you got your basic lead, and that won't get you gelato."

Hawk squeezed the bars again.

"Surely," Minerva said, "a master thief like you can tell the difference."

"That's two down to Kitty Carlisle," Hawk answered.

Again no one laughed.

"Well?" Mayflower demanded irritably.

Hawk hefted the two bars carefully, placed them on the table, and tried to dig into them with his nails. They wouldn't give. He brushed his fingers lightly over their surfaces. He rapped each one with a knuckle. He weighed them again, and finally ripped the blindfold off. The bars were as they had been described, but they couldn't be.

Mayflower nodded smugly: *oh, yes, they are.*

Minerva, sprawled in her chair with that damned dog, waggled her fingers at him. "Cool, isn't it?"

He wasn't sure "cool" was exactly the way he'd describe it. A little unnerving was more like it. Hell, it was downright spooky.

She almost squealed her pleasure at his discomfort. "Weight, feel, malleability—they're all but identical. On the periodic chart of elements, they are but one proton apart. Great minds, Mr. Hawk, worked for countless centuries to turn worthless into priceless."

"Alchemy," Hawk said skeptically. Clowns they were; and fruitcakes.

"Alchemy!" Mayflower echoed proudly. "That is the business term of the nineties, m'man!" He blew a wet kiss toward his wife. "Minerva read all about it in one of those airline magazines about four years ago. I dumped some lira into research and Shazam! we came across a diary by one of Leonardo's apprentices detailing *Le Machine d'Oro*—the gold machine for those folks at home—and the rest is about to become history."

Minerva applauded.

Darwin bowed and blew her another kiss. Had second thoughts, and blew her another one. "Money, Hawkface, isn't everything—gold is. Fuck T-bills! Fuck blue chip stocks! Fuck junk bonds! I got the real thing! Money will always be paper, Hawkie, but gold will always be gold."

Alchemy, Hawk thought; and the goof really believes it.

Minerva cast a grand gesture toward the portrait. "A couple of years of steady production, and we'll flood the market with so much gold that gold itself, the foundation of all finance, will lose its meaning. Brokers, economists, and fellow entrepreneurs will drown in the saliva of their nervous breakdowns." Her eyes clouded in ecstasy at the thought. She hugged herself and sighed. "Markets will crash-crash. Financial empires will crumble-crumble."

"Except yours-yours," Hawk said, catching the drift fast and wishing they hadn't bothered to throw it. "The goal of world domination."

She applauded him without making a sound. "In 1992, Europe is coming together to become one business superpower. It's one party we're going to love to poop."

No, he thought, I don't think so.

In fact, I know so.

As he glanced around the table, he realized that these people were beyond fruitcake, beyond loon, and a good thousand miles into the realm of the truly fanatical. And the absolutely dangerous. All that posing and posturing, all that kiss-kiss, hug-hug crap, Alfred and his magic now-you-see-it-now-you-don't blade—it hit him for the first time that he wasn't going to get out of this alive. They didn't dare let him go home. He knew too much, and he hated that damn dog. Hell, the next thing he knew, they'd probably want him to rob the Louvre or something.

Darwin slapped his shoulder genially as he passed to stand by his wife and squeeze her neck playfully. "Well, all that said, the last ingredient of the recipe is a model of a helicopter."

Minerva giggled. "Which is on display, for three days only, at the Louvre in Paris."

Oh, God! I hate it when I'm right, Hawk thought miserably.

They looked at him.

He shrugged. "As opposed to the Louvre in Wisconsin?"

"Just shut up!" Darwin yelled. Composed himself. "Look, you're gonna make me lose my place." He took a deep breath. "The security will be overwhelming."

Tell me something I don't know, Hawk thought.

Minerva said softly, "Twelve guards."

Twelve? Twelve guards?

With goddamn guns.

"Time out, that's it," he said before they could continue. "Who gives a shit? The Vatican. The Louvre. Why not?" He shut his mouth to stop the babbling, set his jaw, set his mind. "I choose not to accept this assignment. Listen, this is all too Indiana Jones and the Tomb of King Tut for me, man. Just throw me back in jail. And go ahead, just try to throw Tommy—"

"Jail, you asshole?" Minerva shouted, face flushed and fist hard on the table. "Jail? Our foot soldiers will blow your brains out! Bunny! Ballball!" She flung the dog off her lap and pitched a tennis ball at it.

Darwin leaned over the table, teeth gleaming in a shark's smile. "That's right, Hawk, no jail. I'll torture you so slowly, you'll think it's a career. I'll kill your family, your friends, and the bitch you took to the prom."

"You need an address on that last one?" he asked

blithely, then jumped when Bunny snarled at him. "*Et tu*, Bunny?"

The dog barked.

Hawk barked back.

Minerva pushed herself to her feet and shook her head sadly. "You've got a dilemma, tiger, and I think I know what's going to help you solve it."

A signal if he ever heard one, but he was too slow to prevent Alfred from slamming his head back painfully against the chair, stunning him just long enough to slap on the blindfold and the handcuffs.

He felt the heat bubble in his chest, felt it climb behind his eyes. "I'll kill you all," he promised flatly. "Even the old lady."

He kicked the table to shove the chair back, jumped through his arms to bring the handcuffs to the front, and worked at the lock with his teeth, another skill the nuns of St. Agnes would despair of his knowing. And once he was free, he yanked the blindfold away, ready to take on the first idiot who tried to stop him from leaving this madhouse.

The room was empty.

He blinked, looked around, looked back to the exit, and saw Tommy 5-Tone standing there. Not smiling.

At first, he was ready to leap over the table and grab him, kiss him, take him by the throat and demand to know where the hell he'd been all this time.

Then he froze.

Something was wrong.

Tommy moved deeper into the room, winced at the Mayflower portrait, ran a finger slowly across the table's polished top.

"I hated cigarettes until I saw my first No Smoking sign," he said, deliberately averting his gaze from his friend. "Keep Off The Grass? Hell, let's play soccer. Only law I cared about was friendship." He did look then. "Guess I broke that one too, didn't I?"

Hawk started to speak, changed his mind.

Something was really wrong here, and he felt the hairs on the back of his neck vibrate in warning.

"This Gates-Mario-brothers-CIA-Mayflower thing," Tommy went on sorrowfully, "seemed like a sweet deal. Visit foreign lands, take their treasures. I don't know. I thought you'd get into it. It's better than playing darts with MBAs at the bar." He spread his hands to indicate how helpless he was, how mistaken. "But I didn't know it was going to be like this, Hawk. Them using me to use you. Swear to God. I'm sorry, man, but there's only one way out of this, and believe me, it's gonna hurt me more than it's gonna hurt you."

Hawk couldn't believe what he'd heard.

He couldn't believe that his partner, his best friend, practically his damn brother, would betray him.

And he definitely couldn't believe the gun Tommy pulled from his coat pocket and aimed at his heart.

17

It should have been a nice day.

Hell, it should have been a great day.

The piazza outside the Mayflower Building was crowded with tourists, with locals enjoying the beautiful weather, and with music. All over the place you couldn't take two steps without falling over someone playing a violin or a concertina or a guitar. None of it great, none of it terrible. It simply *was*, and made the area more like one vast carnival than a way to get from one street to another.

Horns honking, people laughing, men singing, women calling for their children . . . it was normal, it was wonderful, it was Rome.

It sucks, Darwin thought; and soon enough these people won't be able to breathe without my permission. The notion made him giggle. Minerva turned to him, a quizzical eyebrow raised. He only grinned and kissed her square on the forehead, a gesture that made Kaplan, in that extraordinarily tacky trench coat, scowl in disgust.

They stood in the center of the steps, facing the piazza and waiting for something to happen. From the second they'd stepped outside, however, Kaplan had complained about the plan, thinking it was stupid, and if he had had his way, the both of them would have been wasted days ago.

Which was why, Darwin thought a bit sadly, Kaplan would always wear that idiotic trench coat and I will always wear a Rolex, one for each wrist, not counting the one wrapped snugly around his ankle.

It felt dumb, but Minerva loved it.

Kaplan glared at a street urchin racing behind a fleeing cat. "I just don't think it was a smoking hot idea to leave them two up there alone."

Minerva patted the man's arm in false commiseration. "Don't worry, George. This is the reason we put the old pasta slurper on the payroll in the first place—to keep Hawk in line. Nothing will happen. They'll talk about 'being buddies' and 'chugging brewskies.'" She hugged herself out of a shudder.

Darwin nodded. "Tell you, George, you just gotta love this male bonding."

He slapped Kaplan on the back.

Minerva patted his arm again.

And a window behind them exploded outward.

No one seemed to notice but the trio on the steps, who turned in shocked surprise, then horror, when they saw Tommy and Hawk grappling for Messina's gun.

Kaplan sniffed. "You were saying?"

Tommy regained his feet first, glass and bits of window frame clinging to his hair and chest. He tried to aim the gun but he was still shaken from the fall.

Hawk, meanwhile, panted to a standing position, glared at the gun, and yelled, "You bastard! You fucked my freedom for a lousy *job*?"

Tommy raised the gun, shrugging at the same time. "Hawk, I'm so sorry."

Hawk bellowed incoherently and charged him, butting him in the chest and grabbing him around the waist. They toppled to the staircase and rolled down, forcing Darwin to dance nimbly aside or be snarled in the avalanche that lasted all the way to the ground. Minerva grabbed his arm tightly, and he took her hand while he tried to think what went wrong and how he was going to straighten this mess out.

He supposed, while Kaplan looked to him for instruction and he beckoned Snickers and Butterfingers to him out of the crowd, that the first thing ought to be to get that gun before someone got hurt.

The gun went off.

Twice.

A cloud of pigeons rose from the piazza and whirled into the sky.

Minerva gasped.

Darwin held his breath.

Then Hawk stumbled backward, shaking his head in disbelief, his hands out, pleading. "No . . . Tommy!" He looked around wildly, then dropped to his knees and cradled his friend's head in his lap.

Darwin saw the blood spread rapidly and thickly across Messina's chest.

"Tommy!" Hawk wailed. "Jesus, Tommy, wake

up! We can't go out like this, I still owe you for the tuxedo."

Darwin signaled Kaplan to get down there and do something before it all blew up in their faces, but the CIA man was too slow. Almost instantly a police van shot through the crowd, siren whooping, and braked beside the fallen pair. The doors burst open and four Rome policemen leapt out, one busying himself keeping the crowd back from the scene while two picked up Tommy by the shoulders and feet and carried him swiftly into their vehicle. The last one grabbed Hawk and none too gently hauled him after his dead friend.

The siren whooped.

The fourth policeman jumped into the van as it sped back the way it had come.

Minerva scratched the underside of her chin. "Well. Plan B, George?"

Darwin had no reply.

Kaplan only snarled. "Right. Plan B."

Snickers, however, snapped his fingers at the big man and raced down the steps, shoving through the crowd until he came upon a line of unchained Vespas parked near a curb. He leapt on one and roared off, Butterfingers right behind him. The van had ducked into one of the smaller cobblestone streets that led off the piazza, and he lost it only for a second, but that was long enough.

As he came around the corner, he nearly slammed into the rear of a huge truck that had *Vatican Souvenirs* in red and gold all over it. Snickers skidded to a sideways halt, barely missing two priests in long black cassocks making their pious way down the road. They blessed him absently and walked on, neatly parting when Butterfingers roared around the corner as well, tried to brake, and spread several pedestrians and a flower cart onto the pavement.

"God *damn!*" Snickers said, and coughed when the truck backfired into motion and smothered him with exhaust. "God . . . *damn!*"

The truck kept moving, its driver paying no attention to the two men desperately combing the street behind him. Through a bewildering maze of back streets and alleys he drove without slowing, scattering pedestrians and bike riders with equal fervor. The only time he slowed was when he reached a steep slope that eventually brought him above the city and to a level stretch marked by a low stone wall and a wide pavement where tourists often used up half the film they had just to capture the beauty spread out below them.

The truck stopped.

The driver beeped the horn once.

Anna turned from the wall and lifted her sunglasses as the back doors burst open and Tommy jumped to the ground, laughing hysterically and clapping when he saw her.

"Oh, thank God you're dead," she said with a laugh.

Tommy danced in a circle, waved at Hawk who climbed much more slowly out of the truck.

"It was so beautiful!" Messina laughed. "When the blanks went off, they absolutely freaked!" He spread his hands over his red-stained shirt. "You can't beat Heinz 57."

Hawk stomped up to him breathlessly, took in Anna's presence with a glance, then looked down at his hand, saw it curl into a fist, and saw it move in a graceful, truly satisfying arc right into Messina's jaw.

"You bastard," he said quietly. "You fucked my freedom for a lousy job."

Tommy rubbed his jaw, not sure now whether to keep smiling or not. "But I said I was sorry."

Hawk marched straight to the wall, looked down, decided that there wasn't enough drop to kill him right away. With his luck, he would only bounce a lot over the rocks and through the stunted trees, then end up in some creepy hospital with every bone in his body broken twice; but he'd still be alive.

Out of the business, for sure, but somehow it seemed a little drastic.

He looked back at his friend. "No sweat, Tommy. You only made the biggest mistake of *my* life." He looked up, hearing his voice begin to crack with indignation. "I can't believe you got involved with the Mayflowers. I . . . what was your per diem?"

Tommy stiffened, his good humor evaporated at the insult. "Hey, don't act like you've never committed a crime before, Hawkins. I know, I made a bad call, okay? When Anna tracked me down, I—"

"Hudson," Anna said, "you don't understand—"

He turned on her, making her retreat a short nervous step. "And you, Dr. Cappuccino . . . you're lucky I don't hit women, assuming you are a woman. I'm not taking anything for granted anymore."

With a wave of disappointment and disgust at both of them, he looked back over the city, seeing nothing, feeling everything. What the hell, he thought, broken bones aren't all that bad, and maybe the nurses will be pretty. Maybe I could retire on disability.

Tommy stepped up behind him, Anna alongside him.

"Look, Hawk, I thought we could make this job work for us, you know? It was Anna who made me realize what a stupid pawn I was. I love you, man."

At the same time, in the other ear, Anna said, "I work for a covert Vatican humanitarian organization. The CIA made a fool of me. I care for you."

Hawk shook his head brusquely to quiet them. Replayed what they'd said. Sorted it out and felt a little foolish. "Oh." Slowly he turned to face them, held out a hand and uncurled his fingers. In his palm was the grinning demon's head. "Well then, what's this?"

He didn't much care for the way Tommy shrugged ignorance; he cared even less for the way Anna lost all her color and almost crossed herself.

"Where . . . where did you get that?" she asked, voice trembling.

Another puzzle, he thought; if I'm so good at them, why can't I figure this one out?

"You know," he said. "That place back there where you gave the bad guys the Codex. The Mayflower Museum, or whatever it's called."

She moved closer, examining it without touching it. Hawk was not reassured.

"It's from the machine," she said at last.

He held it close to his eyes, squinted at it, and felt a curious tingling in his palm. "Oh."

Anna's color returned slowly, along with a faint not-quite smile. "So they were really that close to making it work." She reached a hand out toward it, pulled it back, and the smile broadened.

Tommy gave her a quick, one-arm hug around the shoulders. "But now they've lost the services of a certain cat burglar and his 'dead' partner."

She nodded. "They can't get the third piece of the crystal!"

Hawk slipped the demon's head back into his pocket and patted it.

Not bad, he told himself, a little on the accidental side, but you didn't do too badly, Hawkins.

Suddenly he felt as if someone had punched him lightly in the stomach. Not a bad feeling, a friendly tap to get his attention. He looked up into the vivid blue above him and saw a bird, too high to identify, soar effortlessly over the city, and he watched it until it vanished into the sun.

All his life he'd been like that bird, flying around, doing nothing, living off others without giving anything back.

Was that him?

Was that really him?

Folks had tried to tell him, but he was too stubborn to listen to anyone but himself. The nuns . . . he smiled at their memory. They had done their best, and all he had ever done in return was throw their hard work back into their faces.

So what does that make you, Eddie?

What the hell does that make you?

What it makes him, he thought, is retired. Done. Like he'd promised the moment he'd walked out of Sing Sing.

He felt like laughing.

He felt like singing some kind of aria suitable to

the location and the giddy sensation that made his head feel as if he'd drunk far too much champagne.

He turned his back on the city and said, "And now we get to go home."

Tommy nodded. "And we get to go home."

They walked slowly toward the truck as Anna hurried ahead to talk to the driver.

"Tommy," he said, jerking a thumb back toward the wall, "let me ask you something."

"Go."

"Why did they leave all those rocks and shit lying around the yard?"

Tommy shrugged. "They're called ruins, Eddie."

"Ah. Ruins."

Like I used to be, he thought, but this ruin gets to be put back together again. Rebuilt. Modernized. The new and improved Hudson Hawk. Half owner of a classy little place in Hoboken soon to be restored to its rightful put-your-feet-up-and-belch-if-you-want-to glory.

Beautiful.

Absolutely beautiful.

And the best part of it was—absolutely nothing could go wrong now.

18

The plan was simple: they would stay at Anna's apartment tonight and through the next day while she returned to the Vatican and arranged with her people for their trip back to the States. Since Tommy had died so tragically, and so publically, new papers would have to be created, a new identity that would get him through the airports on a somewhat roundabout way home, and past customs inspection in New York.

Which was fine as far as it went, but Hawk balked at the idea that he too would have to travel under an assumed name. He wasn't dead. He wasn't anything but eager to get the hell away from this crazy place and into his own home.

Anna's argument for that was as simple as the plan: if he traveled as himself, when he was supposed to be jailed, it was entirely possible Kaplan would intercept him somewhere along the line.

If he did, somebody was going to lose an awful lot of blood.

Hawk saw the wisdom.

Blood was not good unless it stayed in one's body.

He spent the rest of the afternoon trying to come up with a name that didn't sound like John Smith or Bill Jones—this was his life, after all—an exercise that soon drove Anna out of the apartment to her office, and Tommy mumbling into the kitchen where he scrounged the makings of a simple dinner. By the time Anna returned, with two bottles of wine, Hawk had decided that John Smith wasn't really all that bad.

He had seen Tommy Messina's size-eighty fist threatening his nose.

He had seen the wisdom in not getting too complicated.

He sprawled in one corner of the couch, Anna in the other, and Tommy had taken over the armchair, one leg hooked over the armrest. With no urging at all, they told her about the bar, about the yuppies, about Hoboken, and finally, when Hawk had taken out his wallet to show her a picture of the 5-Tone, they told her about Little Eddie.

It hurt.

But not quite as badly as it had.

In fact, it felt kind of good in a melancholy sort of way.

"So," Hawk said, "when we go up to this hotel room, we open the door and see Little Eddie in bed with this little monkey hooker."

Anna's expression—*sure he was; now pull the other one*—made him giggle.

"She had silk stockings!" Tommy insisted from the chair. "Little Eddie was going steady."

"That monkey had an expression on his face

when he got caught," Hawk told her, making the Boy Scout sign, "that I've never seen on any human being."

Anna stared at him, stared at Tommy, then looked around as if hunting for something to throw.

Hawk laughed, blew her a kiss, and settled back, sighing heavily with the knowledge that soon he would be drinking wine and laughing back in his own place.

It was a good feeling.

"Hey," said Tommy, emptying his glass, setting it on the floor, "speaking of getting caught, isn't the CIA going to think to check out this place?"

Spoilsport, Hawk thought; it's done, man, it's over. Who the hell cares?

But he knew that voice from the old days. Messina was beginning to doubt the course of their good fortune, and if he kept it up, they would soon be barricading the windows, nailing iron over the door, and digging a secret passage through the floor to someplace like Athens, for crying out loud.

"They bought the fake death," Anna reassured him for what Hawk figured was the thousandth time. "And they think Hawk's been arrested." She curled one leg up beneath her, rubbed her ankle absently. "Kaplan and the Candy Bars were seen by my sources boarding a plane out of Rome."

Hawk grinned at him—*see, you old fart?*

Tommy ignored him. "Where to?"

Anna stiffened. "I'm not—"

"For God's sake, 5-Tone," Hawk snapped, "will you please stop worrying?"

Tommy spread his hands. "I'm not worried. I'm just cautious."

Hawk rubbed a hand lightly over his face. Messina in his cautious mode meant they would have to check their shoes for scorpions in the morning. Sometimes he was just like a fussy old woman ... or just like Thomas Messina. Which was sufficient to drive anyone nuts, even the nuns at St. Agnes, bless their evil little hearts.

Another round of wine was poured.

Tommy broke some fresh-baked bread into chunks and passed it around after taking half of it for himself.

Anna pulled the other leg up under her, one arm stretched across the back of the couch.

Hawk looked at her. He looked at Tommy. He wished Tommy would decide to stretch his legs and take a leisurely walk in the lovely summer night's air.

Preferably to Naples.

"Okay," Anna said then, "you have to tell me— why is he called Tommy 5-Tone?"

"That's easy," Hawk said quickly. "There was this guy who lived in our neighborhood named Victor Pinzolo—"

"Excuse me?" Tommy said. "Excuse me? Am I excused? Is it my name?"

"Yes," Hawk said.

"Then it's my name. I'll tell it." He bowed to Anna, took a bite of his bread, swallowed, and cleared his throat twice. "You see, there was this guy, Victor Pinzolo—"

"But everybody called him Pin Head," Hawk said eagerly, chuckling as he remembered. "Because, see, he was this big, loudmouthed dude who was always bossing ..." He saw Tommy's glare, saw the bread crumble in the man's fist.

He shut up.

The trouble was, Tommy didn't know how to tell a story properly. He never could. He always left out the good parts. He opened his mouth, but Tommy beat him to it.

"Hey, if you don't mind?" Messina smiled an apology to their hostess for the uncouth behavior of his obnoxious friend. "Victor, see, made the mistake of hitting me up for some bullshit protection money."

Hawk rolled his eyes. "It wasn't about that. It was about Donna the boffer."

Tommy swung his feet to the floor and shook his head impatiently. "It wasn't about a broad or a boffer, meathead. It was about the money." Another apology to Anna as he clasped his hands between his knees. "So this guy holds out his hand for the dough-re-mi, see, and I was still young enough to be stupid, so I—"

"That's not what happened," Hawk muttered.

Tommy's back went straight. "Eddie, this is *my* name, *my* story. So let *me* tell it."

Hawk raised his hands, palms out in surrender. "You're doing great. Go ahead."

Jerk.

"No, why don't you do it?"

Hawk shrugged.

Tommy insisted.

Hawk knew he didn't mean it, and told it anyway: "So Victor is bugged because Tommy is hitting on his girl. So Victor comes into the bar. Tommy and him are having words, and next thing

I know, Tommy hits him—bam bam bam bam *bam*. Five shots." He illustrated by punching his palm five times. "And for every punch, a tone comes out of his mouth, Victor's, hithertofore unheard of by modern man. Sounds like this . . ." He did his best to duplicate the notes and nearly choked himself. "Tommy 5-Tone." And he hoped Anna understood it was Hawk who had given Messina the label.

Tommy stared at the floor. "My name."

Anna laughed, clearly not believing it no matter who told it, and pushed herself off the couch. "Well, guys, on that note, it's time for bed."

Hawk straightened expectantly.

Ten years.

Ten long years.

Really long years.

"I couldn't agree more." He faked a yawn, stretched, stood up, and pointed at Tommy, then at the couch. "You sleep here."

"What?" Tommy blinked at the effects of the wine. "Where are you going to sleep?"

Silly boy, Hawk thought, and watched as Anna moved about the room, locking the door, closing the shutters over the windows, humming to herself.

Singing, he told himself gleefully, Lord, Lord, she's singing.

When she was done, she headed for the bedroom. "I'll get you some sheets."

Hawk saluted Messina. "Yeah, let's get you some sheets."

Tommy grunted glumly at him.

He winked and hurried into the bedroom. Anna stood at a closet, fumbling inside.

Hawk inhaled slowly. "It's a very special night," he said softly.

"Yes, it was."

His smile wavered a little. "Is."

He moved toward her, leaned forward to kiss her, and received a soft, light, gentle kiss in return. And quick. So quick, he had to think about it before he realized he had gotten it.

"Was," she corrected. "There are things you don't know about me."

"There are things I *do* know about you," he told her, stifling a flutter of panic in his gut. "And about me. And about that bed."

It should have worked.

The soulful eyes, the sincere tone, the strong implication that here was a wreck of a man who had been deprived of the company of women for too long to be natural. And, it went on as she reached into the closet, this man was set up, remember? Sure he was a crook, but he was an honest crook. Used to be an honest crook. Now he was retired. So doesn't he get a gold watch or something?

He got an armful of bedclothes and two pillows.

He looked at them.

He looked at her.

She laughed warmly and turned him around and nudged him toward the front room. "This is not the time, Hudson."

He groaned. "Don't call me Hudson."

She nudged him again.

He looked mournfully over his shoulder. "Can't we just have a late-night cappuccino?"

Her shrug was both touched with sorrow, and

amused. "I'm sorry, but the machine's still set up for poisonous foam."

"Oh. Yeah. I remember."

A final poke sent him from the room.

"Good night," she called quietly.

Yeah, he thought.

Tommy looked at him, grinning like an idiot.

"Not a word," Hawk warned him. "Not one word."

Messina choked back a laugh. "It's a very special night."

Hawk threw a pillow at him, then sheets, and dumped the rest on the couch. When Tommy moved toward it, Hawk stopped him with a glare. "That's it, pal. Hit the floor."

Tommy made a sound almost like a whimper.

Hawk refused to relent. "If," he said, slapping the sheets into place over the cushions, "I ain't getting any cappuccino, and I ain't getting the woman, I am at least getting the goddamn couch."

Tommy laughed.

Hawk threw himself onto his unexpected bed, folded his hands behind his head, and stared at the ceiling.

He sighed.

He was, he realized, doing a lot of sighing lately, and for damn good reason, if he did say so himself. He wasn't sure about the St. Agnes nuns, but he was getting a damn good idea how the damn monks felt.

He didn't like it.

In fact, the more he thought about it, the more he hated it.

He would have to make plans then. Foolproof, guaranteed, ironclad plans.

Tommy began to snore.

As soon as he got back home, he was going to plant himself in front of his door and grab the first woman he saw. Then . . . then . . .

He fell asleep.

And screamed when an excruciating pain snapped him awake, and he found himself face-to-face with Snickers the Candy Bar.

19

Hawk kicked the sheets away as he scrambled up on the couch, the pain fading, sleep destroyed. Unless, of course, he was still asleep, and dreaming. Dreaming, hell; a nightmare. It had to be a nightmare because there was Kaplan and the rest of his jolly CIA crew in clothes that, for God's sake, made them look like fraternity brothers just back from a softball game. Butterfingers even carried a cooler of beer.

Nightmare.

Sure.

Had to be.

These guys thought he was in jail and they had left town. Anna said they had left town. She sat right there and said her sources had seen good old George get on a plane. She said so.

Kaplan sniffed. "The license plate on the police van had a Vatican prefix."

Damn, Hawk thought.

"I'm losing respect for you guys," Kaplan continued. "You were that close, buddy, to getting away with this crap."

So, Hawk said to himself, nothing can go wrong, right? Everything's taken care of and nothing can go wrong. Tommy's too cautious; nothing can go wrong.

You. Are. A. Jerk.

Tommy snored on the floor by the couch.

Hawk kicked his side viciously.

Tommy snored.

Hawk smiled at the others and kicked him again.

Tommy sat up abruptly, scratching through his hair, blinking as he looked around the room and saw the Candy Bars. His expression said *oops*.

Hawk was not heartened.

"Where's Anna?" Kaplan demanded.

Hawk forced himself not to look toward the bedroom. "George," he said heartily, "it's great of you folks to drop by, but next time you should really call ahead."

Anna, where the hell are you?

Tommy picked up on it, pushed himself around so that he leaned back against the couch. "Look, why don't you stop back in half an hour, okay? We'll grab a shower, pick up some croissants and shit—"

Kaplan glared at him. "You know, I really wish I could come up with glib repartee the way you guys can, but I can't." His lips twitched. It might have been a smile. "So I'll just paralyze you. A.J.?"

Hawk's eyes narrowed as Almond Joy pulled what looked like a cigarette holder from one of her pockets. Then, from another, she took out a cigarette case that she snapped open with one finger. She took something out, and Hawk didn't think it was a cigarette, not unless they started making them with nastily pointed tips.

"Curare darts," she said, fitting one into the blowgun.

He tensed to throw himself over the back of the couch, out of harm's way.

"When it comes to instantaneous loss of all physical control below the neck," she said, bringing the blowgun to her lips, "I can't recommend them more highly."

Hawk braced himself.

Kaplan snickered.

Almond Joy spun around suddenly, and Hawk felt a pinprick of pain in his neck. He tried to leap to his feet, and gasped when nothing worked. Not his arms, his hands, his legs. Nothing. All he could do was watch as Messina bellowed to his feet, stiffened, and fell back helplessly.

A moment later they were arranged sitting up, side by side, with their legs crossed.

"We're going to kill you!" Hawk yelled, and feeling rather stupid doing it.

"I'll bite your tongues out!" Tommy snarled.

"Let me get my . . ." Hawk looked down at the rag that was his body. ". . . my teeth at you!"

The Candy Bars laughed.

Butterfingers took a beer from the cooler and drank as he giggled.

Tommy, his face squeezed as if trying to turn it into a fist, twisted his head side to side, glaring at them all. "Come on, you chickenshit sons and daughters of bitches! My head against yours! Fair fight."

Hawk strained, but nothing moved, not even a

toe. "This is how I go out? Like a hunk of Play-Doh? Like some Gumby in a store?"

It was humiliating.

And his rage at being helpless was almost as great as his rage at being caught, almost literally, with his pants down. He should have listened to Tommy's worries; he should have insisted Anna take them someplace else. A hotel. A sewer. But he was only a cat burglar, what did he know from the CIA and sneaking around like spies and shit.

Damn.

Butterfingers laughed loudly, spitting beer over his chest.

"Keep laughing, Jumbo," Hawk said.

Butterfingers roared, then snorted. "Shit, you made it come out my nose."

The Candy Bars laughed even louder, and Hawk took the time to test his fingers and toes again, thinking he felt something somewhere down there, but unable to prove it. He'd just have to keep trying. Curare didn't last forever, right?

Right?

No one answered.

Nuts.

"Look," he said to Kaplan, hoping to stall for time until he could get control again, "George, this is not the way to get me to do the Louvre."

Kaplan lifted an eyebrow. "Hawk," he said, his tone indicating bad news to follow, "the Louvre is yesterday's news. Or should I say this morning's."

He snapped his fingers, and from a corner of the room Hawk couldn't see, Kit Kat emerged. In a Santa Claus outfit. And from his bag he took a newspaper and held it up.

"I admit we displayed a lack of nuance," Snickers said.

The headline read: LOUVRE ATTACKED.

"We didn't wear black; we didn't sing 'Swinging on a Star.'"

Billions in artwork destroyed. Guards slaughtered. Da Vinci Model Missing.

"It hurts me to think that if we had showed Butterfingers here how to aim a bazooka, the 'Mona Lisa' might still have a head."

Hawk was too stunned to say a word.

Butterfingers blushed when Almond Joy tousled his hair.

"But we weren't being graded for neatness," Kaplan said flatly. "Only results."

He reached into Kit Kat's bag, pulled out the da Vinci helicopter, and held it up for Hawk to see.

Hawk felt a prickling sensation in his left leg, something tingling in his right arm. He swallowed, looked at the model so hard his eyes nearly watered.

Tommy nodded toward the newspaper. "Damnit, the Yankees lost again."

Hawk blinked at last. "How'd the Mets do? Could you turn to section D?"

The world tilted then, suddenly and alarmingly. Hawk barely had time to yelp before Butterfingers finished tipping the couch so that they spilled to the floor, lying alongside each other like, he thought miserably, two store mannequins waiting to be dumped in the closet until next time.

The tingling increased.

The prickling eased.

Kaplan stood over them, his face expressionless.

"You guys still might be the fairest cat burglars of them all. Maybe if you weren't such snobs, some innocent guards would still be alive." He shrugged; he didn't give a damn. "It's irrelevant now."

He shrugged again.

"You're irrelevant now."

With a switchblade he sliced easily through the belly of the helicopter and pulled out a mirror Hawk knew immediately was the missing piece of the crystal.

"Tonight, in the castle at Vinci, we make gold."

Hawk strained, and thought he felt his leg move just a little.

"Next month," Snickers said smugly, "in Tokyo, London, Paris, and Moscow, we make financial chaos. This is no joke."

"But this is," Kaplan said. He smoothed the front of his trench coat and cleared his throat. " 'Mrs. Hawkins, can Eddie come out and play baseball?' 'But don't you know that Eddie is paralyzed from the waist down?' 'Sure. We want to use him as third base.' "

The Candy Bars giggled.

Hawk felt his blood pressure rise as he strained to move that damn leg without being obvious about it.

Kaplan examined the blade carefully, then looked down at Hawk, who suddenly wished his throat wasn't so damn exposed.

The door opened.

"Rise and shine, sleepyheads," Anna called cheerfully as she kicked the door closed behind her and, at the same time, tried not to spill the groceries from the bags she cradled in her arms.

"Hi, Anna," Hawk and Tommy said from the floor.

Kaplan turned. "All right! More babes for the party."

There were a lot of legs moving around out there, but Hawk tilted his head so he could see Anna's gaze flick from one crew member to another. Panic momentarily flitted across her face. Then, studiously calmly, she put the bags down onto a side table and opened the drawer.

Hawk blinked.

Anna looked around again, then whipped out a gun and a pair of handcuffs. Kaplan took a step toward her, and froze when she aimed the revolver at his chest.

"Don't be foolish, Mr. Kaplan," she warned, her voice hard, no trace of panic, or fear, at all. "This Bud's for you. Now why don't you give me that crystal?"

Hawk grinned. "Anna Baragli—"

Tommy grinned. "—came to play!"

Sometimes, Hawk thought in relief, life is good even when it looked like hell.

Anna flashed him a smile, then tossed the handcuffs at Kaplan's feet. A gesture suggested that the man pick them up unless he wanted to practice a little bleeding.

Kaplan didn't move; he only smiled.

Almond Joy slid a pace sideways, but Hawk could only see her legs as Anna shifted as well, to stand by Tommy's feet.

"Anna-banana," the Candy Bar said with almost preternatural calm as the gun tracked her, "you're not going to shoot little old me."

He twisted his head again, and saw Almond Joy put the blowgun to her lips. "You're not going to shoot little old anybody. I've read your dossier, Sister."

Before Hawk could shout a warning, a dart settled neatly into the center of Anna's throat. Her eyes widened, the gun fell from her hand, and she fell in collapsing stages until she lay next to him.

"So why didn't you shoot?" he asked.

"I'm sorry, Hudson."

"Don't call me Hudson," he answered automatically. "I told you that only the nuns called me . . ." He cut himself off and turned his head; they were practically nose to nose, and he had to blink to keep from crossing his eyes. "Hey, why did she call you Sister?"

He saw it before she said anything, and made an on-the-spot executive decision that he didn't want to hear it.

She sighed. "I'm sorry, Hudson. I really meant to tell you."

I don't believe it, he thought, the first woman in ten years, a truly gorgeous creature, and she's . . .

He wanted to cry.

"He didn't know?" Snickers exclaimed in malicious delight.

"He didn't know?" Almond Joy echoed.

"Aw," Butterfingers said. "Hawk likes a nun!"

Somebody, thought Hawk, is going to pay for this.

He thought it again when, from a chest of drawers, the two men pulled habits and, giggling insanely, waltzed them around the room while Almond Joy clapped time.

Pay, he thought, and heard a choking noise from

his left, looked, and saw Tommy's face grow a shocking shade of red as he pulled his lips between his teeth and whimpered.

"Messina," Hawk said, "those had better be tears you're crying."

"But it doesn't mean I don't love you," Anna said from his right.

He turned his head to her, feeling as if he were caught in some really bizarre tennis match. "Oh, no, I'm sure you love me. You're a nun. It's your job to love me." The bitterness, and the disappointment, were impossible to hide. "You probably even love Butterfingers."

Anna closed her eyes, opened them. "Well ... yeah ... in a weird Catholic way, I do. But you ... you ..."

Her lips pursed, and quivered.

Hawk reminded himself, sternly, that this was a nun here; stupid and reformed cat burglars paralyzed from the waist down do not, on pain of going straight to hell, kiss nuns.

At least, not the way he was planning to kiss her if he could just get his head close enough.

He could.

But she wasn't there when he got there.

Butterfingers had her draped over his shoulder almost before he realized she was gone.

Kaplan nudged Hawk's foot. "Miss Baragli's da Vinci expertise allows her to go on to the next course."

Hawk kept his face a blank—but he had felt the man's shoe.

"As for you," Kaplan went on, "a little souvenir."

He dropped the ruined helicopter onto the floor and dusted his hands.

Hawk strained, and felt his leg tremble.

A soft grunt beside him—something of Tommy's was coming around too.

Kaplan nudged him again, a little harder. "You know, Hawk, I'd like to think that, in a way, we did this job together. In another life, we could have been friends. But I fear not in this one. You're about to find out how." He grinned. *"Ciao."*

He snapped his fingers and walked out, Butterfingers and Kit Kat trailing behind.

Anna, from the big man's back, said, "Later, guys."

"Easy for you to say," Tommy groused.

Snickers reached into the Santa Claus bag just as the door closed, pulled out a golf bag, then rummaged through it for a moment.

Hawk realized then he could move. The question was, how much and how fast, and what good would it do him? The way he felt now, the aftershock of a sneeze would be sufficient to blow him off the terrace.

"Boys," Snickers said, "we have some good news and some bad news."

Almond Joy leaned down, examined each of their faces. "The good news is, you'll be completely unparalyzed in two minutes."

Don't tell me, Hawk thought.

Snickers did: "The bad news is, that gives you only five seconds to defuse the bombs."

"Bombs?" Hawk said.

"Bombs?" Tommy repeated.

From the golf bag Snickers pulled a rifle of a kind

Hawk had never seen before. An attachment to its muzzle puzzled him until Snickers aimed at the ceiling and fired.

Hawk understood.

Suctioned to the plaster was a bomb.

On the bomb, conveniently placed for those about to die, was a digital timer that told him Almond Joy hadn't been exaggerating—he had less than two minutes and five seconds to live.

20

For a few very brief seconds when no one spoke
once the b-word had been said and the implications
set in, Hawk was convinced that the nuns at St.
Agnes were somehow behind this whole evening's
entertainment. With the speed of divine light they
seemed to employ whenever they sensed something
wrong, and about which they were never ever
wrong, they had learned about his feelings for
Anna, and now they were going to prove to him
that they were right and he was doomed and if he
thought it was hot in Rome . . .

He moved his leg, drawing it up; it felt like lead
had replaced all the muscle.

Beside him a groaning Tommy had done the same
with one shaky arm.

Snickers applauded mockingly with one hand
against his leg as he loaded another bomb on his rifle
and checked its timer. "I'm glad it has to be like this."
He looked to his partner, jerked his head toward the
back. "I'll shoot the other one in the kitchen."

A jaunty wave to Almond Joy, and he turned away.

Not, thought Hawk, a good decision.

With a loud grunt, and all his concentration and a fair amount of prayers focused on his leg, he slammed his knee up into Snickers's crotch. The man yelled and fell where he stood, the rifle leaping from his hand to land on Tommy's chest. Messina instantly grabbed it with his good hand and, without aiming, fired across Hawk's body.

The bomb stuck to the Candy Bar's head.

At the same moment, Hawk scrabbled Anna's fallen handcuffs to his side, rolled up to his knees with more speed than he thought possible, and snapped them quickly on the man's wrist and the leg of the couch.

"A.J.," Snickers screamed hysterically as he yanked frantically on the couch, at the cuffs, tried to pummel Hawk, and nearly broke his shoulder in the twisting. "For God's sake, more paralysis!"

Hawk felt like dying.

He changed his mind, decided he felt like throwing up instead.

But he couldn't move again, not yet, he needed a few minutes, maybe a year or two, before everything worked again.

Meanwhile, shaken by the abrupt explosion of confusion, Almond Joy fumbled her designer blowgun out of her hip pocket, searched for the cigarette case, found it, and promptly spilled all but one of the remaining darts to the carpet. With a curse, she slipped that one into place and whirled to the men lying on the floor.

Tommy moaned something about Hoboken and the bar.

Hawk looked up at the bomb's digital timer face on the ceiling, looked at her, decided this was not going to be a good way to die, and lurched to his feet, whirled, and grabbed the woman's shoulders.

Her eyes widened in surprise.

He covered his end of the blowgun with his lips and blew as hard as he could.

Almond Joy gagged, reeled out of his grasp, and collapsed. "I suppose this," she muttered ruefully, "is what I get for darting a nun."

Tommy used the couch as a crutch to get back on his feet. He swayed alarmingly before finding what was left of his balance, then looked up at the ceiling.

Less than a minute to go.

He looked at the bomb on Snickers's forehead.

Less than a minute.

He looked over to Hawk, who said, "You can move?"

"Yeah."

"Why didn't you tell me?"

Messina tried, and failed, to shrug. A flap of his hand was all he could manage. "I didn't know myself until a few seconds ago."

Without a word, then, they shambled toward the nearest exit—the shuttered terrace window—Hawk gritting his teeth in determination, feeling no pain but knowing that as soon as he looked away from his feet, he was going to fall.

And once he fell, he was going to die.

"Hawk!" Snickers called desperately. "Tommy! Hey, I'm a good guy, goddamnit!"

Open the shutters, Hawk ordered his hands; just lift the latch, open the shutters, get out on the terrace, there are bushes down there. Soft bushes, please, God, he added.

He did it once at the Rutherford; he could do it again.

Maybe.

"Damnit, I'm a winner! An American male winner! College tits on Saturday, Eddie Murphy saying the word 'garbage disposal'!"

Closer.

Tommy swayed and nearly toppled. He caught himself and moaned in fear before lumbering on, bent forward at the waist as though he were battling a hurricane wind.

Hawk refused to look back.

The terrace was all that mattered.

"I got to get a new job," Almond Joy said calmly.

Half a minute, maybe less.

Hawk didn't want to check.

"Oh, God," Snickers moaned, thrashing about wildly, trying to haul the couch up high enough to slip the cuffs off. "I always wanted to learn how to play the harp. There was just never enough time. Rosebud!"

Tommy grunted. "Man's going to give himself a migraine."

Hawk reached out for the latch, blinking hard, sweat dripping into his eyes, his lungs feeling as if they were trapped in a wet cotton blanket. His hand slipped away just as the front door slammed open.

"Buon giorno!"

Hawk glanced over his shoulder and decided that this wasn't your ordinary get-out-of-the-apartment-before-it-blows-up kind of day. And if the nuns weren't behind it, the devil sure as hell was.

Standing on the threshold, fat as ever and holding a gun, was Antony Mario.

Son, he thought, of a bitch.

It almost made him stop to ask how in hell the man had gotten out of the ambulance alive.

Almost.

Ten seconds.

Maybe less.

Antony swept over the room with a cold, intimidating stare. "Nobody fucks with the Mario brothers and lives," he announced loudly. He looked at Hawk and smirked. "You didn't think I would find you, huh?" Then he saw the woman lying helplessly on the floor, and Snickers by the couch, with the bomb attached to his brow. He scowled. "And who the fuck are you?"

Hawk looked at the ceiling.

There was no time left.

"Maybe," said Snickers hopefully, "it's a dud."

In your dreams, Hawk thought, whirled, and crashed through the shutters, staggered across the terrace with Tommy right beside him, and looked down.

The bushes were there.

He wasted no time, but immediately threw himself over the railing just as Antony called in a confused voice, "Hey, where's everybody going? I just got here."

Flying, Hawk thought deliriously, I'm flying, and I'm safe.

The apartment blew up.

Hawk never saw the ground.

* * *

Darwin Mayflower had always adored his Treasure Room at the castle. All that luscious gold, all those obscenely huge jewels, the artwork and the statuary, the dizzyingly exquisite delights of a dozen Fabergé eggs—it made him tingle all over just to think about it.

Until today.

Today, just when he had the world snuggled cozily in the palm of his hand, ready to be crushed as soon as he felt like it, matters were beginning to look a little on the dicey side as far as the timetable went. Not that he minded all that much. He'd straighten it all out, no problem, he was a Mayflower.

But it was the damned inconvenience of it all.

It was really starting to piss him off.

The good news was that the stupid Jersey Italian bar owner and his overrated cat burglar ex-con buddy were now just so much cat food in a Rome alley left behind when the apartment building blew up.

The bad news was the condition of Dr. Baragli.

No sooner had Butterfingers brought her in and had her strapped to one of his favorite antique chairs—worth a fair million and a half to the right sucker with a checkbook—than she had drooled extensively on the embroidered upholstery. Then she had blown him a kiss not even Minerva could duplicate when she wore her black leather kilt with the studs around the hem. Then, when he was about ready to scalp her and say the hell with it, she had giggled loudly in such a high-pitched voice that he thought his eardrums would burst.

It was almost like the sixties all over again, only this time there was no sex or rock 'n' roll. Just drugs.

He demanded an explanation.

Minerva, as usual, offered none.

Kaplan, as always, looked as if he could not, even at the cost of his life, care one bit less. "Well, I don't know," he said when Darwin asked him for the tenth time what the hell was going on. "This curare we've been using, it sometimes has side effects."

Minerva looked to Anna. "You don't say, George."

Anna's head lolled on her shoulders. She burped. She excused herself. She looked dreamily up at the gilt-edged ceiling and said, "I feel like ... like a dolphin that's never tasted melted snow."

Darwin took his patience in hand, resolved to remember that she was a woman and a nun, and walked over to her, ignoring a signal from his wife not to strangle the bitch before they got what they needed.

Strangling was out of the question.

A good beheading, on the other hand, would cap the evening off nicely.

"Now listen carefully, Anna," he said, a loving but stern father to a zoned-out daughter not yet beyond redemption, "the apprentice diary contains a code that explains how the three pieces of the crystal fit together." He smiled disarmingly and wiggled his fingers behind his back. "If you would do us the honor of deciphering the code ..."

A door opened.

Anna grinned stupidly toward it.

Alfred wheeled in a silver-filigreed serving cart on whose top shelf was the ancient diary, the two crystal pieces, and the mirror.

She blinked rapidly and giggled. "What does the color blue taste like? Bobo knows." The giggling stopped. She looked at each of them in turn and announced, "I have to talk with the dolphins now."

Go ahead, Darwin thought angrily, then talk with the lions, the tigers, the whales, I don't give a shit as long as you talk to me next!

Her mouth opened.

He waited.

She shrieked.

He stumbled backward, staring openmouthed until he realized she was trying to imitate the voice of a dolphin.

Son of a bitch, he thought, this is a nun?

Minerva raised a hand. "Just shoot her?" She looked around. "Anybody?"

Darwin was almost inclined to agree.

"Darwin. Darling. This is supposed to be torture, not therapy."

"Torture?" He turned to her, his arms wide, his face toward heaven. "Can't you see what kind of pain I'm in?"

He looked back at Anna.

All right. Enough's enough.

One more peep out of her and he'd turn her over to Alfred.

She grinned absurdly, and peeped.

Darwin took a deep breath and signaled the English assassin.

21

Hawk remembered very little about what happened after the explosion. Landing in the shrubs had been a piece of cake considering his condition; on the other hand, ducking all the flaming debris had awakened his muscles quicker than any possible antidote. By the time he had slapped out the embers on his clothes and moved as quickly as he was able down the street, the sidewalks were filled with exclaiming, terrified neighbors.

No one stopped him.

No one stopped Tommy.

Before long, the night was filled with wailing sirens, a secondary explosion emptied the streets as fast as the first had filled them, and he was ready to sit in the gutter and take his chances with the fire trucks.

He was tired.

He was more than tired; he was exhausted.

And he was aching again.

Just when he thought all the bruises and bumps

and cuts and gashes had left him alone, their cousins returned, with a vengeance. It was enough to make a guy go crooked again.

Then he realized he was alone, spun around in a panic, expecting to see Messina sprawled on the pavement, his old heart finally given up the ghost.

What he saw was Tommy slipping blithely into the front seat of a small Italian car, bending over, and the engine firing up a few seconds later.

Amazing, he thought as he ran to the passenger door, the man's absolutely amazing. Hidden talents and a yuppie bar. Amazing.

When Tommy looked at him for instructions, he almost told him to find the nearest airport, seaport, or cross-Atlantic tunnel, don't spare the horsepower and don't run the stop signs. Almost. Unfortunately, the moment the words prepared themselves for delivery, he thought of two damn good reasons why he was thinking like a jerk.

Anna was the first one, and no explanation necessary.

The second was the Mayflowers. And Kaplan. And all those damn thumps he'd taken since he'd walked out of prison what seemed like a hundred years ago.

His hands curled into fists, his eyes narrowed.

It wasn't fair.

Set up to do ten years, blackmailed, jumping around the damn world like a puppet and no way to cut the strings just because he was good at what he had done.

It wasn't fair.

He thought of Anna again.

He thought about the world, what it would be like if Darwin got his way.

He stirred uneasily, feeling Tommy watch him, knowing that his friend was probably reading his mind and waiting.

Damn.

He wasn't a hero, for crying out loud. He was just a guy, that's all, nothing special.

It just wasn't fair.

On the other hand, nothing was fair, right? People like Anna and Tommy get duped and dumped on all their lives, and people like Darwin Mayflower and George Kaplan walk all over them with perfect impunity. Money talks, dignity walks. The meek don't inherit anything but lousy crumbs, and the Darwins of the world have written the damn will.

So maybe he could do something.

Maybe not.

But he knew, with a horrid sinking feeling, that he'd never sleep right again if he didn't at least try.

Oh, hell, Eddie, he thought, you're in for it now.

They drove for what had to be forever, through deserted streets, streets packed with automobiles and trucks, streets teeming with pedestrians who thought they were running the bulls at Pamplona, and finally a highway that spun them away from Rome and into the country.

He didn't ask if Tommy knew where he was going. Messina had never gotten lost in his life. One look at a globe and the man could find his way blindfolded across Siberia on cross-country skis.

Hidden talents.

Amazing.

Several hours later he suggested to his friend that they just might have crossed over into Switzerland. They'd certainly been driving long enough, and he had seen, thank you very much, enough vineyards and olive trees to last him pretty much the rest of his life.

Tommy growled at him.

Hawk pointed at the dashboard and suggested they stop for gas before they ended up walking. And while they were there, he added innocently, maybe they could ask for directions. Or pick up a map.

Tommy growled at him. But stopped.

It was Hawk who, with a lot of hand gestures and enough body English to throw the peninsula across the Mediterranean and into the African continent, discovered that Vinci was off to the west, and had they been following the right roads, they would have made it there by lunchtime.

He growled.

Tommy shrugged and said what the hell, they weren't going to kill Anna so what's the big deal?

Hawk glared at him—*drive or die.*

Tommy drove.

And it was dusk when they slipped into a valley and the Vinci castle finally rose above the horizon.

Hawk grinned. His directions were perfect. Tommy, however, had seen fit to contradict him at every pasture, cattle crossing, and well.

"I'm telling you it was a right," Messina complained, pulling off the narrow road at the base of the castle's hill. He cut the engine and folded his arms across his chest.

"All right, all right." Hawk peered through the

windshield at the high walls, the towers, the closed main gate, and all the uphill land between the road and their destination. "Besides, that's not what I'm worried about."

"What are you worried about?"

Hawk pointed at the hill, the rocks strewn across its face, and the gullies that crossed it. "I'm worried about you. You sure you're up for this climb?"

Tommy leaned away from him. "Climb? Are you kidding? We're fifteen minutes from the castle gate. We can drive there."

Hawk looked at the rocks, the gullies, the slope, the even narrower road that wound easily up it.

"I knew that," he said. He nodded. "I knew that."

Halfway to the gate, however, they changed their minds. It would not, they decided, be a good thing just to drive up as if they were visiting old friends. Climb it would have to be. Or take the chance of being zapped by one of Kaplan's mystical weapons.

The car was stowed off the shoulder, behind a huge bush, and Hawk led the way around the slope, angling upward and wishing he had thought to bring hiking boots, proper pants, a heavier coat, and a Sherman tank. By the time they reached the base of a turret and he sagged against a drain pipe, he was panting.

Gasping.

Then gaping at Tommy, who stopped beside him and propped Snickers's golf bag against his leg.

He didn't ask.

He didn't want to know.

But the thing, he thought, had better have some goodies in it or I'm gonna own the bar outright before dawn.

Tommy, red-faced and puffing, grinned at his expression. "Does that mean you're not going to help me carry it the rest of the way?"

Hawk puffed his cheeks. *"Andiamo,"* he said, and picked up one end while Tommy, still grinning, picked up the other.

Heavy.

The bastard was heavy, and that meant goodies.

They stumbled around the castle's irregular base for what seemed like hours, despair slowing them down as they realized there was going to be no convenient way in, no unlocked door, no unlatched window. There was also the cliff that the castle clung to. A very high cliff.

Nuts, he thought, they were going to have to think of something else.

"Nuts," he said as they rounded another corner.

Tommy stiffened. "What happened?"

"I got mud all over my good shoes."

"How much did they cost?"

"Four hundred bucks."

Tommy grunted.

Hawk trudged on.

The sun dropped lower, gliding shadows into the valley and across the slope. The temperature began to drop as well, and a haze lifted from a distant river.

Hawk knew it was futile to just keep walking around like this. The place was too damn big, and they had no idea how to get where they were supposed to be even if they did manage to climb over the wall. What they needed was some kind of sign, a signal, a miracle, a light in a tower window just like that one over there.

Damn, he thought, the kid's still got it again.

And *damn* again when they reached the tower's base.

He grinned and stopped.

Tommy looked around, puzzled. "So where do we go from here?"

Hawk pointed. "How about we climb these convenient cables they got here?"

Heavy cables, slipping from the turret high above their heads. Electrical cables. Meaning they had, for a change, run into a bit of luck.

Tommy slung the golf bag over his shoulder and rubbed his palms briskly. "On the count of three?"

"Why not just go in?"

Messina shrugged.

Hawk looked at him, looked at the thirty or forty feet they had to climb to what looked like a ledge just below the turret wall, and began to wonder. He knew he would be all right; the cables were rough, easy enough to grip without slipping. His buddy, on the other hand, was not in the best of shape. Or size, for that matter.

"So, you ready?" Tommy asked eagerly.

"Tommy."

"What?"

Hawk looked up again. "Better let me go first."

"Damnit, will you stop worrying about me?"

"Who's worrying about you? I don't want you to fall on me with that damn bag."

Without waiting, he dried his hands as best he could on his pants, grabbed hold of a cable, and began to climb, using the stone for a foot grip as he would if he were climbing a mountain.

It was higher than he first thought.

But he didn't look down, and this time didn't try to tease Tommy about the distance between them and the ground.

Tommy said nothing as well; only his soft grunts proved he was still down there.

Hawk's arms began to tremble from the strain, his legs suggested strongly that he give it up, the tower was too high, and just about a third of the way he heard voices over his head. He didn't stop. He didn't dare. One second's rest would undo him. He had to go on.

The fingers of his right hand began to cramp, and he took his weight on his left while he shook the cramp away.

Tommy grunted, feet scraping against the stone.

Only a few feet from the top, Hawk heard the voices again and knew who it was—guards. The son of a bitch Mayflower had posted guards on a tower a zillion feet above the earth and a zillion miles away from the nearest human being. What was he expecting, some kind of raid from the air?

Jesus.

Anger propelled him then, and the last few feet were as easy as the first. It wasn't until he was crouched on the ledge that he understood exactly how high he was, and the vista spread before him was gorgeous as twilight cloaked the valley, and dizzying enough to churn butter in his stomach. He looked away quickly and helped Tommy climb aboard. Then he peered over the top of the low wall and saw two men in Mayflower World Tour baseball caps and satin jackets whispering to themselves while trying to light cigarettes in the steadily blowing wind.

Swell, he thought as he ducked back down and hand-signaled his find to Messina, swell.

Y'know, he thought further, shifting his weight when Tommy let him know they would have to do a charge before they got blown off, Superman didn't have trouble like this. He didn't give a damn about rifles and bombs. He even had a cape. I don't have a cape. If I'm supposed to act like goddamn Superman, why the hell didn't anyone give me a cape?

Tommy pulled himself into a crouch.

One of the guards asked the other one if he had heard something.

Hawk sighed.

Thought one two three, and leapt over the wall.

Just as the guards turned around, their guns aimed straight at his head.

22

Darwin decided that he would, without question, accept any one of a half-dozen categories of Nobel Prize, and there would be no false modesty involved simply because he deserved it. Anyone would after dealing with a spaced-out nun who wanted nothing more than to commune with dolphins and make pigeon noises at George Kaplan.

If, as Minerva had had to remind him more than a few times, they didn't need her translation of the diary so desperately, he would have dumped her out the window two hours ago.

As it was, the Nobel Prize for Peace Among Batty Nuns would do just fine.

For now.

At the moment, he and his wife, and Kaplan the idiot, were waving the three pieces of da Vinci's crystal in front of Anna's eyes, hoping that somehow they might bring her out of it. He prayed it would be soon. All that conversation with her celestial dolphins, while no doubt stimulating, was giving him a splitting headache.

"A lifetime of service has come to this," Kaplan complained to no one in particular.

Minerva snarled at her. "The dolphin is dead. The dolphin is ... oh, for God's sake, come on, you bitch."

Anna, who seemed to Mayflower not quite as high in orbit as she had been, sighed morosely. "I'm not a very good damsel in distress, am I. 'I can't pay the rent.' 'You must pay the rent.' "

The dolphins returned.

Darwin snapped his fingers not an inch from her nose. "Yo, Flipper! A damsel in distress implies that there is some well-hung Dudley Do-Right galloping up to save you." His voice dropped to a harsh growl. "It ain't gonna happen. Hudson Hawk go boom-boom. He ... is ... dead."

Kaplan turned to the window and shook his head doubtfully. "I wouldn't be so sure." He checked his watch, the window, his watch a second time. "It's absurd that Snickers and Almond Joy haven't reported in yet."

Minerva rolled her eyes. "George. Don't be a bore."

Kaplan ignored her.

He couldn't take his eyes from the window, and the night darkening outside.

Hawk slipped into his satin jacket and snapped his baseball cap twice against his leg before putting it on. Not the best of the assault ensembles he might have chosen, but at a distance, in a pinch, with everyone else blind, he and Tommy just might, maybe, pass for guards until it was too late.

The guards themselves had passed off the tower some time ago.

When he was ready, and shivering against the chill the setting sun left in its place, he looked around the tower floor and groaned. "Hey, Tommy, shouldn't we have taken those guys' guns?"

Tommy struggled with the golf bag. "No thanks," he said with a you-ought-to-know-better tone. He pulled out one of Snickers's time-bomb rifles. "I've been thinking of using a seven iron myself."

Hawk looked around the castle, its walls, the grounds below, and tsked. "Looks kind of long."

Tommy shouldered the rifle, practiced his aim and holding the weapon's weight. When he was satisfied, he said, "Mind if I play through?"

Hawk spread his arms. "Please do."

Tommy bowed with a gracious nod of his head. "Don't mind if I do." He looked around, grinned, and yelled, "Fore!"

Hawk winced. "Tommy!"

"What?"

He fired.

Hawk watched the bomb arc through the air toward the lawn below and to their right. "Did you set the timer on that thing?"

Messina frowned. "No."

Great, Hawk thought.

"Look, from now on, would you please set it?"

If nothing else, he added silently, it will give us time to get away before we end up flying ourselves back to Jersey. Or parts of us anyway.

Nevertheless, he plucked another bomb from the bag and, after a few seconds' fumbling, locked it on. Made a show of setting the timer. Brought the rifle quickly to his shoulder and was glad they had decided not to try to hit anything specific, just make a lot of noise and trouble; he doubted he could hit the broad side of a barn from inside the way this damn thing wobbled around. In fact, he'd be lucky if he didn't blow off his damn foot.

Hang on, Anna, he thought then; hang on, darlin', the cavalry is here.

Kaplan could see nothing through the window, turned away from it and looked across the room. The Mayflowers were still unsuccessfully trying to drag the woman back to the planet.

"Fore?"

The Mayflowers looked at him, then frowned at each other.

"Did anybody hear anything?"

The first bomb exploded.

Butterfingers raised his hand. "I heard something, boss!"

I am blessed, Kaplan thought.

With one hand buried in his pocket, he started for the door. "Come on, Butterfingers, let's move it. Kit Kat," he called over his shoulder, "you guard the Mayflowers with your life."

Kit Kat saluted and moved to stand in front of Anna, who began to wish the dolphins would come back. But she had bid them a fond farewell just about the time something large and loud had exploded outside the window.

She looked up at the mime.

He looked down without smiling.

A faint noise distracted her then, and she saw Alfred ghost out of the shadows with a crossbow in hand. A huge crossbow. An astonishingly elaborate one that had been customized to hold two bolts, to have two triggers.

"Plan C, Alfred," Darwin said, lovingly placing a Robin Hood cap on his wife's head.

The Englishman handed Mrs. Mayflower the weapon.

Anna gaped.

"Oh, Kit Kat," Darwin called sweetly, "are you really going to guard us with your life?"

"Kit Kat!" Anna warned, struggling with her bonds, then freezing when he held up one of his cards.

I know, it said, but he couldn't turn in time.

The bolts caught him one on either side, and he flipped another card between his fingers—*ouch* —before pitching forward onto her lap.

She almost screamed.

She almost screamed again when she felt his hands moving swiftly around her.

"A double crossbow for a double cross!" Alfred announced calmly, as if calling the score of a tennis match.

My God, she thought, the man's dying, and he's copping a feel.

"Oh, Alfie," Minerva cooed. "You dry British madman."

Then she felt the knots loosen and fall away, felt Kit Kat stiffen, and she bit her lower lip to keep from crying out when he looked up at her, smiled secretly, and died.

Darwin applauded. "Is there any mammal we can't screw?" He chuckled proudly. "Alfred, the shortcut." Then he winked at Anna. "Catch you on the flip side, baby."

Anna finally found her voice as Minerva strode past her behind her husband. "Why . . . why did you do that?"

Kit Kat slid to the floor.

Minerva stopped and looked at the dead man. "Try this one on, Sister: Thou shalt not share."

A second bomb exploded, and dust sifted down from the ceiling.

Minerva smiled at her and began to reload.

Die, Anna thought, abruptly sad; oh, my God, I'm going to die.

One of the castle weather vanes vanished in an explosion.

"It's in the hole!" Hawk cried. "The gallery is ecstatic! He's got to be happy with that one, Tommy."

Tommy looked down.

Hawk looked down.

Below was a wide terrace that ended at the edge of the hill, the part of the castle they hadn't been able to get to when scouting it earlier. There were wandering paths as well, lawns, shrubs, and the Mayflower limousine parked and pointed toward the main gate.

"Two and a half minutes to save Anna, three and a half to save the world," Tommy told him as he locked in another bomb and shot it over the roof above them.

"Six," said Hawk automatically. He thought. He sifted through his files. "Oh." Another pass. "Oh! 'Side by Side.'"

A beat while he picked up his rifle and reached into the bag for a bomb.

Then Tommy fired. "'Oh, we ain't got a barrel of money.'"

Hawk loaded. "'Maybe we're ragged and funny.'"

"'But we'll travel along.'"

He fired.

"'Singing a song.'"

Tommy fired.

"'Side.'"

Hawk fired again as the castle began to sprout gouts of flame and smoke.

"'By.'"

Tommy grinned and pointed down—*time to go.*

"'Side,'" Hawk finished.

And ran.

George Kaplan was beginning to find Italy not a nice place to visit, much less live in. Castles, for example, were supposed to be strong, safe, above all the fuss and bother of the everyday world. But he and Butterfingers were having a hell of a time trying to find an area where things were not blowing up all the time.

Not that the big oaf was complaining; he thought it was all kind of pretty.

They burst out of the castle onto a path, shoulders hunched when a distant explosion flared orange light over the grass.

It was, he thought, almost like the old days.

Except that in the old days, he was the one doing all the blowing up.

They broke into a slow trot, peering into the shadows, up at the walls, until they came to a fork.

"Let's try down this way," Kaplan said, pointing to his right.

A bomb blew a tree to matchsticks.

"Maybe," said Butterfingers, pointing to the left, "we better go this way."

"Okay, that way," Kaplan agreed as the stump of the tree blew up as well.

This was nuts, Messina thought. We'll never find her this way. We could be running around all night, pass her, and never know it.

He checked the facade of the main building, the wall they stood against, and shook his head. "Okay, let's split up," he said at last. "I'll take the front nine, you take the back nine, and we'll meet back in the clubhouse."

Hawk patted his stomach. "Hey, Tommy, looking good."

A bomb blew on a nearby roof. Tommy thought he saw two guards taking flying lessons.

"Thanks," he said, and slapped his friend's shoulder to send him on his way.

When he had rounded the corner, Tommy snared another bomb and began to hook it to the rifle.

" 'But we'll travel along,' " he sang softly, " 'singing a song, side by—' "

He stopped.

Someone appeared out of the dark.

Oh, he thought.

" 'Side,' " said Alfred, flicking out his knife. He reached for the rifle. "I'll take that, sir."

23

Hawk didn't hear Tommy finish the song, but that was all right. Not two seconds after he'd left, he had an idea. It wasn't much of one, certainly not without its flaws, but it was better than running around in the dark, so to speak, hoping for another miracle to drop Anna in his lap, and the Mayflowers off the nearest cliff.

What he had to do was get to the room where he had seen what he now knew were the unreconstructed pieces of da Vinci's gold-making machine. It was the only place in the castle he knew, and where he suspected they might be holding Anna, since she held the key to its instructions.

And if she wasn't there, she would probably be nearby.

Close enough, he thought, for jazz.

He slammed inside, sprinted down a corridor longer than a runway, skidded around a corner, and thudded painfully against a wall, glared at it, and ran on, reached another corner and slowed down so not to make the same mistake twice.

He heard voices.

Eureka, he thought, pressed against the wall, and looked down the connecting hallway. Oh, mother, Eureka.

George Kaplan stood by a doorway with his back to Hawk, Butterfingers beside him, looking more than a little frazzled.

"Butterfingers, go in and brief the Mayflowers of the current situation."

"You got it, Coach."

Hawk held his breath, tried to make himself invisible, and slipped into the hall as the Candy Bar entered the room; the room, he realized, that must hold Anna.

Kaplan sniffed, shifted his weight from foot to foot, stretched his neck, sniffed again.

Hawk sidled along the wall, debating whether to kill the bastard first and then ask questions, or ask questions first and then shove a bomb down his throat. It was going to be a close call.

The door opened.

He froze as he heard Minerva giggling delightedly, and widened his eyes when Butterfingers came out and closed the door carefully behind him. There were things in his chest. Lots of things. Things, he recognized, like the things you shoot out of crossbows.

"Coach," the big man said mournfully, "I think the Mayflowers must have set us up." He sighed, and pitched forward onto his face.

Hawk stepped up beside Kaplan and looked down

at the fallen warrior. "Ah, Butterfingers, we hardly knew ye."

Kaplan stiffened. Turned slowly.

Hawk smiled.

Kaplan shrieked, lashed out with a foot, and as Hawk leapt out of the way, he had an unpleasant feeling this wasn't going to end in the first minute of the first round.

Anna found it difficult to breathe, much less speak when Minerva, once again, demanded an interpretation of the diary so they could get on with destroying the world and get home. First there was Kit Kat, whose body had been dragged out of sight to a corner; then Butterfingers came in, beaming, and Minerva had punctured him several times without saying a word.

Now it was her turn.

Minerva loomed over her and demanded a response.

Anna shook her head stubbornly.

"Well," the woman said, "since you're not going to tell us what we want to know, I think it's time for you to report to the home office in heaven, Sis."

Anna reminded herself she was a nun. A pacifist. A gentle person who couldn't even shoot a despicable person like George Kaplan when said despicable person had rendered Hudson and Tommy weak and helpless.

Nun.

She was a nun.

Minerva gloated, then sneered. "If you talk to the Big Guy, tell him for me that He's a loser."

Anna stared.

Minerva stared back.

"Oh, that's it," Anna said, and sprang up from the chair, grabbed Minerva, and gave her a head-butt that put stars in the room.

Minerva toppled.

Anna ran for the door, ran back and grabbed up the pieces of da Vinci's crystal, and ran back to the door. She had no idea where she was going, but anyplace was better than here.

Tommy figured he had but one chance to survive, and since John Wayne was dead, so was he.

He had been shoved into the back of the May-flower limousine, and before he had a chance to pick himself up off the car floor, the lights went on, and Darwin himself grinned as he aimed a silencer-adapted pistol at his head.

"Tommy, you New-York-Italian-father-made-twenty-bucks-a-week sonofabitch, you were hired as bait, and on this simple task you have betrayed me. Do you have an answer why?"

Tommy figured something else—dying on his knees wasn't the way his mother, rest her soul, would have wanted him to go.

"I have," he answered grimly, "five of them."

A desperate lash of his foot knocked the gun from Darwin's hand, and before the man could move, Tommy was on top of him, pounding his thick skull with an even thicker fist.

"One," he grunted. And punched.

A note, not quite within human ken, rang through the car.

"Two."

A second note.

"Three."

The third one had sort of an unearthly, but pleasant, New Age ring about it.

"Four."

Tommy's lips pulled away from his teeth.

Not even Hawk knew the name of this one.

But Darwin snared his wrist before the fifth, and fatal, punch was delivered, twisting around so that the hand was placed against the mouth of the shredder. Tommy struggled, but Darwin was too quick.

He turned the shredder on.

Tommy howled and threw himself back, his elbow catching the siren's button. The moment it turned on, Tommy grabbed Mayflower's head and yanked it and him across the seat and jammed the man's ear against the speaker.

Darwin bucked, his hands flailing for Tommy's eyes, for his throat, for anything to give him purchase so he could lever himself away.

One hand found the gun.

Alfred, behind the wheel, glanced into the rearview mirror. "Shall I cut off his head, sir?"

The gun went off.

Alfred grunted.

A knee rammed Tommy's stomach, and he fell to the floor, took a kick to his head as Mayflower grabbed for the door handle, yanked it, and scrambled out. Poked his head back in and said, "Alfred, I won't be needing the car anymore."

Dazed, his ears ringing and his gut aching, Tommy tried to roll to his hands and knees, but the door slammed in his face.

Then Alfred turned around, blood smeared across

his front, and said politely, "Ta ta," before starting the engine, and pressing a button that locked all the rear doors.

Tommy wondered where he was going.

Alfred didn't stick around long enough to tell him. He grabbed up a time-bomb rifle from the front seat, jumped from the car, and released the hand brake.

Panicked, Tommy whirled to look at the rear window just as the Englishman fired his bomb onto the trunk.

This, he thought, is not a good thing.

This, Hawk thought, is getting ridiculous.

After the first dodge, Hawk had tried a series of quick punches to Kaplan's jaw, but the man was too quick, and too quick on his feet as he raced through the castle and up a tower staircase, screaming something about Hawk's supposed death and why wasn't anything going right tonight.

Hawk didn't sympathize.

The stairs were steep, his lungs were protesting, and when they reached the open air above the castle grounds, there were enough explosions right, left, and overhead, to turn the night into a Fourth of July fireworks display. Pieces of stone, mortar, and wood beams were scattered across the turret floor.

Kaplan ran straight to the wall, and Hawk thought he was going to jump.

No such luck.

The man whirled, using the wall as a brace as his foot came around in a blurred arc meant to take off Hawk's head. Hawk grabbed the foot and twisted the ankle savagely.

Kaplan grimaced. "Damn, does everything have to be so hard?"

"Tell me about it," Hawk said, tried to take the foot off, and took a punishing blow to the cheek instead. He fell back, charged before the man could steady himself, and managed to wrap his hands around Kaplan's throat. Which would have been a good thing if Kaplan hadn't done the same to him, spinning them into a mutual strangulation dance that ended only when the CIA agent caught Hawk's shin with the point of his shoe, making Hawk fall backward, breaking both their grips.

Hawk gasped for air.

Kaplan punched him hard enough to lift him off his feet and dump him against the wall.

Hawk staggered to stand. "That didn't hurt," he said, and mentally crossed his fingers.

"Then try this," Kaplan said, and tried another kick.

Hawk rolled clear, the kick hit stone, and Kaplan yowled as Hawk grabbed up a piece of charred wood. Now, he thought, it's the top of the ninth, the bases are loaded, and the Jersey Slugger is going to knock one right the hell out of the park.

They circled each other warily.

An explosion brought more debris to the turret.

Hawk swung.

Kaplan's answering kick took a piece of the heavy beam and sent it over the wall.

Hawk swung again.

Another piece flew through the doorway.

Hawk looked at his slowly shortening weapon.

"What are you trying to say, you centrally intelligent scumsicle?"

He swung.

Kaplan kicked, and stumbled backward, panting.

"Getting old, George?" Hawk said, and instantly took the advantage, catching the man a glancing blow on the temple.

Home run, he thought excitedly.

"Thank you," Kaplan said.

Foul ball, Hawk thought glumly, and couldn't dodge the foot that splintered the last of the makeshift bat and nearly unscrewed his head. He staggered against the wall, shook his head to clear it, wished he hadn't, and moved in to throw a series of perfectly timed, beautifully aimed, superbly executed punches.

They missed.

Kaplan's didn't.

Hawk was beginning to feel as though, maybe, he was a little bit outmatched here.

Kaplan punched.

Hawk dodged, and punched, and missed. "Damnit, George," he complained, "stand still."

Kaplan refused to oblige.

He kicked.

Hawk leaned away from the arc, leaned forward, and his baseball cap fell off. "Hey," he said, "my hat."

Kaplan unleashed a vicious, flying charge.

Hawk bent over to pick the cap up and felt the agent soar over his head.

"I hate you!" Kaplan screamed as he glided over the wall.

Hawk watched his trajectory reach a point where,

for just a second, the man seemed suspended in midair. Quickly he reached into his pocket, pulled out a picture, licked its back, and slapped it onto Kaplan's forehead. "Say hello to Little Eddie, you motherfucker," he said.

And Kaplan fell.

And footsteps racing through the doorway made Hawk groan. He couldn't do it. He couldn't fight anymore. Even his eyelashes were hurting this time, and he didn't care who the hell it was, he was going to surrender and spend the rest of eternity pushing up Italian daisies.

It was Anna.

"Hudson!" she cried.

They embraced quickly, but Hawk winced when she squeezed too hard. "Hey, what's up. We're supposed to be saving you."

"Sorry," she said. "I was bored. I saved myself."

Figures, he thought, fight the dragon, blow up a castle or two, and the princess saves herself. It figures.

"Well, we still got to get those crystal pieces."

She grinned and showed him her hands. "Got 'em right here, cowboy."

"Oh," he said glumly. "Got 'em right here." Suddenly he cocked his head. "That sounds like Tommy."

Anna laughed and punched his shoulder, which he wished she hadn't done, although one broken bone more or less wouldn't matter at this stage. Then he frowned and looked over the wall.

And gasped.

The limousine careened across the castle grounds, heading for the terrace, and the drop beyond. He could hear Tommy inside, screaming for help, and saw Kaplan sprawled on the hood.

"My pension!" the agent shrieked.

Anna grabbed his hand tightly as they watched in helpless horror while the limousine shattered a stone vase, splintered a table, and flew off the terrace.

It seemed to move so slowly.

Flying.

Like a bird.

"Tommy!" Hawk wailed.

The limousine blew up.

Hawk fell against the wall, looking down and not seeing anything until, in a shadow just below him, he saw Mayflower putting away a cellular phone.

Darwin looked up, blinked in mild surprise, then looked out toward the darkness where his limousine had been. "Friend of yours?" he asked.

And Hawk howled his rage, leapt from the wall, and slammed Mayflower to the ground.

"Hawk!" Anna cried.

He looked up, he looked back, and had no chance to duck when Alfred introduced him to the butt of his rifle.

24

Hawk was exhausted.

Worse than that, he was weary.

He hadn't paid much attention to what had happened after Alfred had stunned him with the rifle. The fight had seeped out of him. Everything he had done, and all the people he had killed, had been for nothing, and he didn't much care what happened anymore. Even Anna's presence wasn't enough to stoke the fires again. She had scarcely spoken, defeat had settled in her eyes and her behavior, and try as he might, he couldn't summon the energy to comfort her.

I am not happy, he thought miserably. I was not happy before, and I am not happy now. I'm worse. I think, if it's all the same to you, I'd like to wake up now.

Nothing happened.

Nuts.

Alfred had walked them purposefully but with haste through the halls, into the workshop where,

Hawk now noticed, nothing had changed, except for the addition of a curious-looking bat-wing glider and the tennis-ball machine, and into the cavernous room.

The sheets were gone.

Oh, my, he thought, oh, hell.

In the center of the floor was what he supposed was a machine. But a machine unlike anything he'd ever seen before. It was huge, and it was old, and it was so convoluted in its construction that his eye was unable to follow one level to another. There were levers that didn't seem to lead to anything they might work; there was a huge gear-and-wheel affair that didn't seem to turn anything; and there were what seemed to be hundreds of mirrors and lenses tucked inside and extending outside and sitting on the top, none of which had anything to do with anything else that he could see.

To focus on that could make him believe, at least for the moment, that he had been transported back to da Vinci's time; and it might have done so had it not been for the bank of computer terminals off to one side, manned by white-smocked technicians who wore headsets and holstered guns. They bustled about both the machine and the computers, adjusting here, watching scrolling diagrams there, all in an unnerving, efficient silence.

My God, he thought, they're going to do it. They're really going to do it.

The realization was less like a blow to the stomach than a blow to his pride. This . . . this *thing* was here because he had tried to fight on too many fronts at once. Not, he admitted quickly, that he had known what all the fronts had been. That part

• 225 •

hadn't been his fault. Who knew that a nun could look so sexy? Who knew that the Mafia would throw in with the CIA? Who knew? Hell, he sure didn't.

But he did know this: all of them had a role in murdering Little Eddie and Tommy 5-Tone.

For that, and that alone, maybe he still might take one last chance to derail the Project.

And if not . . .

To the left of the machine, in partial shadow, he noted someone coming toward him. Two someones.

Minerva and Darwin, grinning like idiots.

"God," Darwin said, "I love happy endings!"

Minerva kissed him, giggled, and looked over to them. "You're probably wondering why you're still alive."

The thought had occurred to him, but Hawk wasn't about to question what may or may not be luck.

She ruffled her husband's hair, and absently fondled the goggles and headset dangling from her neck as if they were matched pearls. "We didn't want you to go to hell without knowing that our dream came true." She smiled. She chuckled in embarrassment. "Besides, we are still having some trouble putting that damn crystal thing together. Alfie and I've been going at that damn thing all night."

When a grim-faced armed technician returned to bring Hawk to the table beside the gold machine, he decked the man without looking away from his captors, and without shaking his fist in agony. How the hell, he wondered angrily, do they do it in the movies?

Minerva looked pained.

Hawk stiffened stubbornly. "Why should I help you go for the gold?"

"Why do I have to give you a reason?"

Not bad, he thought, makes sense.

"Hawk, you're just a schmoe."

Now that's bad, he thought.

"You're every schmoe! Every schmoe has the fantasy that the planet revolves around them. It rains, a car crash stops traffic, you say, 'How could this happen to me?' It's a natural inclination. But for me, this isn't a fantasy, it is reality. You are on *my* planet! You walk around the corner for coffee, out of my sight, you do not fucking exist! The lives of schmoes like you have meaning only in relation to the rich, to the powerful, to *me*!"

Hawk pointed at her. "Well, if you put it that way, Minnie, how can I resist?"

Anna laughed sarcastically, hand on her hip. "Yeah, how can he resist? That's a good one, Hudson. If you think we're going to help—"

"Oh, shut up," Hawk snapped. "There's no reason to fight anymore. They're a force of Nature." He glared at her. "And do *not* call me Hudson."

He looked coldly away from the dismay that crossed her face and walked over to the table, picked up the two crystal parts and the mirror.

"If you pull this off," Minerva said anxiously, "I won't promise I won't kill you. I mean, who are we trying to kid? But I will spare the Flying Nun here."

Hawk shifted the components in his hand, weighing them, trying to follow their contours. "And to think I thought you were Evil Incarnate in pumps."

She beamed.

He fussed with the crystal pieces, the mirror, noting how easily they bent, yet how rigid they felt. It nearly spooked him to know that a man—a genius, yes, but still a man—could have created something like this. Nevertheless, he twisted them, fit them, pulled them apart and fit them again. His concentration blocked all sound. His focus saw nothing but the beauty of the piece he was putting together. These things were only a part of a whole, and until he had the whole pictured in his mind, he wouldn't be able to do a thing with them.

He grunted.

His hands moved in a flurry.

He shook his head in exasperation and lifted the pieces closer to his eyes.

His hands.

Still nothing.

He sensed impatience from the Mayflowers, but knew they wouldn't interrupt him.

He held the pieces at arm's length.

He placed them side by side in one palm and tried examining them from several different angles.

Then, holding his breath, from several different angles at the same time.

Suddenly he saw it, the whole that da Vinci had created, and suddenly his fingers were able to tweak this corner here just so and push that corner there just a little, and an explosive *snap* suddenly filled the room.

Minerva immediately snatched the completed crystal from him, pulled on a headset, and said, "Oh, Hawk, don't ever change!" She turned to her crew. "Go, team, go!"

As if presenting a rare jewel to an exacting qreen,

she placed the crystal reverently into the machine, withdrew her arm, and stood back. The technicians left their computers and began their phase of the operation: one of them picked up a long steel pole with which he, delicately and with scowling attention, began to adjust the series mirrors and lenses, a touch here and a harder push there, moving his way up through the levels of the machine to those set in the top, finally adjusting the main mirror installed in a frame that lifted it a good six feet above the construction itself; the other two, following printed diagrams they held in their hands, carefully poured and sifted vials of precisely measured bubbling liquids and colored powder into various slots and troughs around the complicated periphery and in the machine's heart.

It took several minutes, during which Minerva darted from one place to another, checking, rechecking, muttering into her headset and goading her crew into working faster, faster, but completely without error.

Hawk watched it all with a careful eye, and when activity was at its height, he sidled over to Anna, whose glare did its best to turn him to stone.

He only gave her a quick smile.

Minerva stepped back, her posture announcing that it was all done, all but the last step. She turned to her husband and curtsied.

Darwin stepped up to the machine, turning a lead bar over several times in his palsied hands, then took a deep breath and placed it in its niche just below the crystal.

Minerva applauded.

Darwin backed away.

Hawk covered Anna's wrist with one hand.

Minerva took hold of a lever, announced giddily to the room, to the world, "We're for real!" and pulled the lever down.

25

Hawk had to admit that the whole thing was pretty damn impressive.

There was an expectant pause once the lever had been pulled, a prolonged silence and absence of motion.

Then, with a great internal cough and thunderous grinding of gears, the gold machine shook itself and began to rotate. Its movement was sporadic at first, jerk and stop, jerk and stop, until it seemed to find its own rhythm. Then it picked up speed, its revolutions smooth. Arms unfolded from within, reaching out toward the ceiling, then turning inward again. Brass tubes gleamed, their hooded lids opening to allow the spill of chemicals to enter.

Clearly visible in the center was da Vinci's crystal, nestled in a bath of light, slowly spinning counterclockwise to the machine's own rotation.

Minerva stood before it with her hands clasped beneath her chin, her eyes gleaming in adoration, her mouth open, lips quivering.

Darwin, his head snapping side to side before a hand clamped it still, watched the machine warily.

Once the machine began to move, the three technicians had retreated to a video monitor, frowning in concentration, jotting notes on their clipboards, consulting with each other, every so often pointing to a number as digital time clicked off at the bottom of the screen.

Damn impressive indeed, Hawk admitted, then pulled his hand away from Anna's wrist, taking the handcuffs with him. When she didn't notice, he tugged her arm.

She looked at her hand, looked up at him, and her lips twisted in angered disappointment instead of pleasure. "Well, you should be proud of yourself," she scolded acidly. "The machine and the destruction of the world's economy seem to be coming along quite nicely."

He followed the arc of one of the arms as it swooped in stages to within a hairbreadth of Minerva's head; she didn't even flinch.

"Thanks," he said. Another arm carried something small and pulsing in toward the crystal, dropped it, and pulled out. "But tell me, what would happen if that little mirror came out of the crystal?"

Anna waved him away nervously. She had clearly not forgiven him, and stupid questions weren't going to help. "Believe me, you do not want to know."

One of the technicians rapped the monitor with a fist, leaned closer, and peered at the screen. His colleagues leaned closer as well, and they jotted more notes more furiously.

Minerva threw out her hands as if she were a priestess imploring her god.

Hawk held out his left hand. "I do so want to know."

Anna glared at him.

He shook his hand to make her notice it.

She did.

In his palm was the mirror.

She grinned. She fairly shook with delight. She looked at Minerva and the machine and shook her head. "Things are going to get very interesting very fast, my man. Da Vinci would have been proud of you."

A technician looked back at her.

She smiled.

He looked away.

She reached down at her feet and picked up the steel pole.

As Hawk watched her draw the pole back, he knew for sure she was really a nun. Soft one moment, tough as stone the next. And never, ever, without a clear sense of purpose.

It was spooky.

The ingredients, chemical and powder, flowed out of the brass tubes into troughs of their own.

The machine turned.

Arms reached and retracted.

The bar of lead began to rotate.

The crystal glowed.

The ingredients reached a common spilling point, directly over the lead.

There was a hesitation, barely perceptible, before they poured.

A blinding flash filled the room, and an explosion within the heart of the machine. Though it was clearly part of the process, it made everyone jump and cover their eyes.

A cloud of smoke billowed into the room.

Minerva waved a hand grandly toward the machine and crowed, "We're mythic!"

Minerva patted her hair, adjusted her gold costume, and walked confidently into the cloud.

And still, the crystal glowed.

Anna adjusted her grip on the pole, moved Hawk back with a bump of her hip, then swung the pole squarely against the skulls of the technicians at the monitor. They fell as one. The monitor winked and jumped.

Hawk was about to congratulate her when a movement at the corner of his eye made him turn.

Mayflower, somewhat hazy in the smoke now filtering out of the room, raised his gun shakily. "Such disrespect!" he chided over the growing noise of the machine. "It'd break my fucking heart . . . if I had one." What was left of his mouth tried a grin. "No more Mr. Nice Guy!"

"My turn," Hawk said to Anna when the man's first shot plowed into the door.

She gave him a be-my-guest sweep of her hand just as Darwin fired his second shot. It hit the ceiling.

Hawk picked up the pole and held it at his shoulder. Darwin tried to stop his gun hand from shaking by gripping his wrist with the other, but before he could fire a third time, Hawk used the pole as a javelin, slamming Mayflower in and through the shoulder.

The pole caught in one of the largest gear wheels.

The machine turned.

The wheel turned.

Darwin shrieked as the pole lifted him off the ground.

Hawk shuddered and turned away.

"God, can we talk about this?" Darwin cried.

Anna turned away as well, but they could still hear the crunch of Mayflower's bones as the wheel meshed with its gear. A moment later the pole clattered onto the floor.

The crystal glowed more brightly.

The machine revolved more quickly, and began to emit a flare of light beams that spun dazzlingly around the room.

Each beam caught a mirror and intensified.

The mirrors directed the beams up and through the machine.

Their speed increased.

The machine began to hum.

Hawk pulled Anna down and away from the paths of the beams that seemed more like lasers searching for a target. They couldn't be looked at directly, and their intensity was painful even to glimpse. One had crossed his face in a split second, and he was still partially blinded. When he closed his eyes tightly against a second one and tucked

her face against his shoulder, he had a bad feeling
Anna had seriously underestimated the signifi-
cance of the crucial mirror's absence.

Using his free hand as a tentative shade, he
peered through the haze and saw Minerva stride
peacock proud away from the machine. She flung
away her goggles with a flourish and applauded,
giggled insanely, spun around, and cheered when
the lights completed their dizzying circle to the top
and converged on the highest mirror.

A flare.

A sun was born.

Hank threw up his hands.

The machine roared, spun even faster, and the
sun was reflected straight down into its heart.

The room shook.

Anna pulled away so that she could see for herself.

Minerva screamed her joy as the light faded, replaced by a brilliant golden glow where the lead
bar had been.

She whirled and cried, "Eureka, motherfuckers!"

The machine began to growl.

Hawk decided that the show was rapidly drawing
toward its climax and he didn't really need to see
it in person. He knew how it was going to end. A
quick signal to Anna of his intention, and she
agreed readily.

Keeping low, still squinting against the vivid
light growing in the machine, they started across
the floor.

And stopped when Alfred planted himself in their way.

Actually, it wasn't so much Alfred himself that made Hawk straighten and stare; it was the fact that the Englishman, the very proper Englishman, opened his shirt to reveal the words *Rule Britannia* scrawled across his chest. Hawk wondered if this was how all butlers ended up.

"How," the man said.

"Your turn," Anna said without hesitation.

He looked at Alfred, looked at Anna. "My turn? I just killed Darwin."

Alfred coughed. "How dare you take from me the pleasure of killing my boorish employer." A hand into his pocket; it came out with a knife. A long knife whose shaft was hinged. His thumb flicked a lever. The blade snapped out. Seconds later, another knife in the other hand. "It's your first time dying. I'll try to be gentle."

"Definitely your turn," Anna repeated, backing away.

That's right, Hawk thought, you get three guys with their backs turned, I get a butler whose tea has gone to his pointy little head.

Swell.

There was, however, no chance to argue—Alfred uttered a bloodthirsty howl and charged, and Hawk skipped deftly out of the long blades' way, jabbing the assassin's stomach, dodging, jabbing again, dodging. Frustration made Alfred's lunges too predictable, then made them wild. Jab again. Dodge. Hawk wished the man would take the hint and fall down before somebody got killed.

They circled each other.

Alfred stabbed, Hawk dodged and jabbed, and Anna fumbled a gun from the holster of a fallen technician.

At last, the cavalry, he thought gleefully, and rapped his knuckles against the butler's nose.

Alfred howled his rage.

Anna fired.

Hawk stared at the crease that appeared along his arm.

"Sorry!" she called.

Alfred tried to come in low, but Hawk swung an uppercut that glanced across his forehead and drove him aside.

Anna fired.

Sparks flew from Hawk's belt buckle.

"Jesus!" he screamed. "Stop helping me! Thou shalt not kill, damnit!"

He might have said more, and in more colorful language, but Alfred took the distraction to kick Hawk back against the wall, then lunge after him. Hawk barely managed to deflect the knives with a desperate swipe of his arm, and the blades skidded against the stone, angling them so that Alfred, grinning, was able to press the now V-shaped double weapon against Hawk's throat.

Hawk, one hand on Alfred's wrist, muscled his way away from the wall, but his lungs were laboring overtime from lack of air, and the two-blade combination would, he knew, soon force a painful, and messy, separation of mind and body.

Alfred's face reddened with the effort to keep Hawk still.

Hawk's face reddened with the effort to catch a decent breath.

The machine began to thunder.

Dark motes began to float across Hawk's vision.
Alfred's breath was hot and sour.

Hawk tried to concentrate, shifting his gaze from
the mad look in the assassin's eyes to the gleaming
metal that, for some reason, seemed to have his
name etched across them. He realized with a gasp
that he had one chance, and only one chance, to
turn it all around.

He shoved.

Alfred shoved back, strongly.

And in that movement, Hawk twisted the man's
wrists, reversing them, thus inverting the V to en-
close Alfred's neck instead of his. Momentum spun
them around and across the floor, and Hawk
slammed the man into the open door, the points of
the blades dug deep into the ancient wood.

He hesitated.

He thought of Little Eddie. Tommy.

He said, "Excuse my crass American humor,"
and slammed the door.

The force of it freed the points.

But Alfred fell, his wrists and knives still crossed.

The blades slammed together.

Hawk waved at the bloody object spiraling up toward the ceiling. "But hey," he called, "don't lose
your head over it."

The machine's speed grew more frenetic.
Its thunder increased.

* * *

Alfred's head fell to the floor and rolled past Anna, who looked down and said, "Alfie, looking bad."

At that moment, the gold machine's heart exploded and spat a tongue of molten gold right into Minerva's face.

Hawk grabbed Anna's hand, and sprinted with her out of the room, down the hall, and into the workshop. He ran to the window, to the balcony, and looked out and down.

Too far to jump.

The castle began to shudder.

He could hear the machine grow from thunder to earthquake.

When Anna yelped, he ran back inside and saw Bunny snarling and spitting at her.

He grinned. "Your turn."

Anna laughed, looked around for something to use to clobber the little bitch, and screamed when Bunny leapt for her throat.

Immobile in amazement, Hawk watched her fall, but when he finally shook himself and raised the gun, he realized he wouldn't be able to shoot without hitting her.

A piece of ceiling collapsed in the corner.

He tossed the gun aside, cursed himself for tossing the gun aside, and ran after it. Came up short when he saw the tennis-ball machine.

Anna screamed while the dog snarled and growled its way closer to her throat.

Hawk set the dial to its highest level and aimed it across the room.

"Bunny!" he called. "Ball-ball!"

The dog backed away from Anna, its muzzle

touched with gleaming droplets of blood. It looked at Hawk, trembling in anticipation.

Hawk flicked the switch.

A tennis ball shot from the barrel, Bunny jumped, caught the ball, and flew through the window and over the balcony.

Hawk preened.

The gold machine blew up.

So did the castle.

26

Enzio Gramaldi, whose ancestors had been merchants in this valley for several hundred years and, he thought sourly, probably had the same damn mule, climbed down off his long-eared, thick-headed steed and dropped wearily onto a tree stump. The mule wandered off.

It was a beautiful day. A perfect day.

He took a deep breath, and broke into a spasm of coughing that ended only after he'd thumped himself a dozen times on the chest.

What the hell, he thought, and dragged a small wineskin from inside his shirt.

He sighed.

He lifted the wineskin to his lips.

A violent explosion sent wine cascading over his face, his clothes, and he glared up at Vinci castle. Smoke poured from the ruined battlements, debris pattered like rain across the hillside, and the birds in the olive trees flew shrieking into the sky.

"Che pazzo," he muttered.

The mule ran.

Gramaldi stared at it, sighed, looked up, and froze.

The wineskin slipped from his hands unnoticed.

A bird. No, not a bird. A giant bird. No, not a giant bird, a . . . a *thing* that looked like a bird glided in ever-decreasing circles toward him.

He couldn't move.

The *thing* flew over the trees.

He crossed himself.

The mule kept running.

The *thing* became a glider, and the glider landed perfectly on the road in front of him. Two people emerged from under the tattered wing, smiling brightly at him, their clothes sooty and torn, their hair singed, their faces dark.

Nervously he smiled back.

The man asked directions to the nearest village.

Gramaldi pointed dumbly.

The woman—and such a beautiful woman!—blew him a kiss.

They walked off, and he watched them until they topped a rise and vanished beyond it.

Then he stood, whistled for the mule, and walked in the opposite direction. It wasn't his original destination, but he didn't care. Mules he could put up with; people who obviously weren't Italian and flew out of exploding castles he didn't want to know about.

Ever.

He had gone only a few paces when something told him that those people might be injured. They might be hurt. They might need a ride and pay him for it.

He vacillated between greed and his need to find a new place to live, until a large smoking stone landed not ten feet from where he stood.

He whistled for the mule, turned around, and ran.

He was too late.

For them.

Hawk laughed, looked up at the sky, and knew now that he was, indeed, a hawk. A Jersey hawk, to be sure, and from Hoboken, for God's sake, but no one else had flown as he had. And no one else ever would.

Anna came up beside him, and he slipped an arm around her waist, grinned at the sudden convergence of the village's children at the site of their landing, and walked with her toward the plaza.

He had done it.

He had really done it.

Lord, the nuns would be proud.

A lurch in his heart, in his stomach, and he looked at the woman walking beside him.

He stopped.

She stopped.

I will, he thought, definitely go to hell for this; and he kissed her.

Amazingly enough, she kissed him back, and he wasn't sure but that he heard some sort of celestial choir singing, with a little giggling, behind him.

Unless it was the kids.

"Hey," he said.

She smiled.

"Will you play Nintendo with me?"

He held his breath until she answered, "I can't think of anyone I'd rather play Nintendo with."

He smiled. He stopped smiling. "What about your boss?"

Puzzled, she looked around them. "What boss?"

Not puzzled at all, he looked directly into the sky. "You know."

She placed a hand tenderly on his cheek. "I think he'd want me to keep an eye on you."

They walked on, into the square, Hawk feeling not quite real, and not quite sure he was really awake. It was weird. But it beat Sing Sing all to hell and back.

"You know," he said, "I don't know whether to Lambada or Vogue." They headed for a café, its tables sheltered by large umbrellas. "I still can't tell the difference between Tab and diet Coke."

Anna poked him playfully. "It's one of life's eternal mysteries, Hawk. Just be glad you have a life." She nodded toward the café. "Can I . . . buy you a cappuccino?"

He grinned. "Lady, can I kiss you?"

A quick kiss.

Ten years.

Anna steered him to a table, sat him down, put his cup in front of him. Then she took her own chair and suddenly, inexplicably, she sighed.

Hawk looked down at the cappuccino, looked up at her, and did not want to ask. Not now. Not when he was so close.

"I just wish," she said sadly, "Tommy were here."

He nodded, ashamed that he hadn't thought about Messina since they'd escaped the gold room. Then he looked up and over her shoulder.

"No way," he said, standing.

"That's not very nice," Anna scolded.

Hawk grinned. "No way!"

He stepped away from the table as Tommy Messina rode up on a mule, clothing charred and smoking, face scabbed, bleeding, but still in one piece.

They embraced as the big man said, "Did I miss anything?"

When he winced, Hawk sat him down, stared at him, and shook his head in wonderment. "You're supposed to be crashed up at the bottom of the hill!"

Tommy laughed. "Air bags. Can you fucking believe it?"

"But, Tommy," Anna said, "you're also supposed to be blown up into fiery chunks of flesh!"

Tommy's face reddened with more laughter. "Sprinkler system setup in the back. Can you fucking believe it?"

Hawk couldn't stop gaping. "But you're supposed to be dead!"

For just a moment, Messina frowned. Then smiled. "Look, I was supposed to die in so many different ways, the good Lord couldn't decide which one to pick."

Hawk opened his mouth, shut it, leaned back and nodded. "Yeah," he said, "that must be it."

Anna pointed. "Hawk. Drink your cappuccino."

"But shouldn't we get him to a hospital?"

"Eddie," Tommy said sternly, "drink your coffee!"

He picked up the cup.

He waited—for the lightning bolt, the earthquake, the flying saucer that was going to kidnap him and take him to Venus where terrible experiments would be performed on his battered and bruised body.

Nothing happened.
He smiled.
He relaxed.
He looked up and said, "Here's to Little Eddie."
And he drank.
For the first time in ten . . . long . . . years.